A

IF ONLY
FOR ONE
NITE

Other titles by the author

B-Boy Blues
2nd Time Around

IF ONLY FOR ONE NITE

JAMES EARL HARDY

alyson books
los angeles | new york

MANUFACTURED IN THE UNITED STATES OF AMERICA.

THIS TRADE PAPERBACK ORIGINAL IS PUBLISHED BY
ALYSON PUBLICATIONS INC.,
P.O. BOX 4371, LOS ANGELES, CALIFORNIA 90078-4371.
DISTRIBUTION IN THE UNITED KINGDOM BY
TURNAROUND PUBLISHER SERVICES LTD.,
UNIT 3, OLYMPIA TRADING ESTATE, COBURG ROAD, WOOD GREEN,
LONDON N22 6TZ ENGLAND.

FIRST EDITION: AUGUST 1997
FIRST PAPERBACK EDITION: MAY 1998

02 03 04 05 **a** 10 9 8 7 6 5 4 3

ISBN 1-55583-373-X (CLOTH)
ISBN 1-55583-467-1 (PAPERBACK)

LIBRARY OF CONGRESS CATALOGING-IN-PUBLICATION DATA
    HARDY, JAMES EARL.
        IF ONLY FOR ONE NITE / BY JAMES EARL HARDY. — 1ST ED.
        1. AFRO-AMERICAN GAYS—NEW YORK(STATE)—NEW YORK—
FICTION. 2. AFRO-AMERICAN MEN—NEW YORK (STATE)—NEW
YORK—FICTION. 3. CLASS REUNIONS—NEW YORK (STATE)—NEW
YORK—FICTION. 4. GAY MEN — NEW YORK (STATE) —
NEW YORK — FICTION. I. TITLE.
    PS3558.A62375I38 1997
    813'.54—DC21   97-15477 CIP

COVER DESIGN BY MATT SAMS.
COVER PHOTOGRAPHY BY DINO DINCO.

FOR MY, FOR YOUR
SECRET LOVE

Thank U Once, Thank U Twice,
Thank U 3 Times

God, 4 Lovin' Tuff ("Who is He? The First, the Last...the Future, the Past").

My Family & Friends, 4 givin' tuff.

My Fans, 4 readin' tuff.

The New Skool Crew, 4 hangin' tuff: Alaric Wendell Blair, Tony Carr, Lorenzo Bo "Knowz" Coleman, Reginald "Tree Trunk Legs" Harris, Rolando "Honey Cone" Herts, Landis "Outlandish" Osborne, Allyson Reid, Second Sunday, Linus and Gregory Spiller-Kraft, and George B. Walker Jr.

Oleta Adams, Erykah Badu, Blackstreet, Norman Brown, Tracy Chapman, Groove Theory, Roy Hargrove, Phyllis Hyman (*U R missed*), Maxwell, Me'Shell Ndegéocello, Ann Nesby, Joshua Redman, Seal, Cassandra Wilson, the *Waiting to Exhale* Divas, and, of course, Randy and Luther, 4 sangin' and signifyin' tuff as I took that trip a third time (and it was a *trip!*).

&

Mitchell Sylvester Crawford, 4 speakin' tuff.

Memory Lane

Ten years. *Ten years.*

One hundred twenty months.

Three thousand six hundred fifty-two days.

Eighty-seven thousand six hundred forty-eight hours.

Five million two hundred fifty-eight thousand eight hundred eighty minutes.

And an obscene number of seconds that must total in the billions.

Yeah, that's a long time, but it doesn't seem that long. I don't feel as if I've aged a decade (even though I don't know exactly what a 28-year-old is supposed to feel like), and, looking back, I still fail to see how so many years could pass and I didn't notice. But that, they say, is the point: You are not watching a clock as you live, for if you are, then you are not living. Birthdays come and go, and it's all just a part of that evolution, that bridge we continue to cross as we get older (and, hopefully, wiser).

But it's still kind of scary; it's like your life has passed you by. Of course, they say your life really passes you by when you are about to die (yes, about to, since the only people who have been able to actually say this are folks who have been *this* close to death but survived), but I don't believe it. Well, I *do* believe that the people who have experienced such a thing actually have. But I *don't* believe it is something that happens to all of us. It would seem to be a cruel joke — and *He* couldn't have that wicked a sense of humor, you know?

Think about it: You're bleeding to death, your body is racked with pain, you're taking your last breaths, everything is going dim, you can feel the life slipping out of you, slipping away from you, your heart is beating slower, slower...*slower*...and then, FLASH!, this *was* your life, revisited, redressed, replayed for your viewing pleasure? I *don't* think so. In my opinion the people who have these Technicolor flashbacks *want* to have them — in other words, they are so deter-

mined not to die that they dredge up all those
memories as if to remind themselves that, even
though they may have lived a full life, it can't be
over yet because there is still so much they
haven't done, haven't seen, haven't said. This
trip down memory lane gives them that one
extra push, that fighting spirit, and — what do
you know? — *they're back*. But I'm quite sure
there are those who have had such a visitation of
spirits but still left us.

One doesn't have to wait to die to see his life
flash before his eyes, though. Case in point: my
high school reunion. Yes, I graduated ten years
ago this month, and when Pooquie told me
about it and gave me the invitation, *it* happened. Right there, on the spot. I touched the
invite, and then...

Mr. Reid

...the faces of my fellow students...

Mr. Reid

...the school building, the grounds...

Mr. Reid

...the classrooms...

Mr. Reid

...the cafeteria...

Mr. Reid

...the auditorium...

Mr. Reid

...the hallways, which were either populated with too many students or desolate after the bell rang. The stairwells too...

Mr. Reid

...and the...the...gymnasium...

Mr. Reid

...*Oh*, the gymnasium...

Uh-huh...Mr. Reid.

Who is Mr. Reid? Well, I really don't want to get into that right now. In fact, I don't want to get into him until I have to, and I know I'll have to. But not right now, okay?

Anyway, my whole life (in high school, anyway) came back to me in a flash — and then I became depressed. Why? Well, this was just one more reminder that I was, as my younger brother, Adam, has teased me about, "gettin' up there." I'm pushing thirty, I have a boyfriend in his very early twenties, and I'm at a crossroads when it comes to my writing career (well, it feels more like a dead end). Having to face my past at a high school reunion when I'm trying to make sense of the present and what the future will hold...it's just a bit too much to digest (let alone face).

But as the elders say, *He* never gives you more than you can bear. And while he is a glorious reminder of where I have been, Pooquie also reminded me that I've accomplished a lot in the past decade and that I shouldn't feel that what I have done and what I am right now isn't jood enough (it also helped that this pep talk was delivered lying in his arms). I already knew this, but it made me feel better hearing it from the man I love.

Of course, I would've felt even better if he came to the reunion with me. Deep down I know he wishes he was in the space to do so. But it was rather fitting that he had a special date planned that night with his son, Junior, who was making us all proud graduating from kinder-garten. Pooquie's being absent would be a good thing for me, a blessing of a different kind: I lived those high school years without him, and if there were any demons to exorcise — and both of us knew that there were — I'd have to make that trip myself.

So I started that journey by trekking to my mother's home in Jersey. I searched the attic and located my yearbook. Lord, can pictures tell a story: Things looked so much simpler back then — and they were. In those days school was truly a safe haven: We didn't have to worry about walking through metal detectors or being raped, robbed, stabbed, or shot. And do styles come and go: Gloria Vanderbilt and Jordache, snorkel and pea coats, Converse and Puma sneakers, and those ugly unfashionable Cazal glasses (one thing I pray does *not* come back).

When I found my photo, I held the book up to a mirror. Uh-huh, I hadn't changed at all. In a way I was kind of disappointed: You know, you *expect* to age after ten years, you expect to see the signs. The hair is always the culprit: It's either thinning out or breaking out or graying out or just plain *falling* out. But every single one of the hairs I had when I graduated remained (which surprised me, because I've been through a whole lot of shit in the past ten years). But even if I were a Hair Club for Men member, that couldn't begin to tell the story. The places I've been, the people who have come in and out of my life — you wouldn't be able to figure out what I've been through or where I am by studying the surface.

Some of my classmates also fell in this category; others didn't.

Myles Hatfield and LouEllen McCoy. Picture a teenage Opie and Pippi Longstocking. If their ancestors did have those bloody battles in the hills of Appalachia in West Virginia, that was certainly all in the past as far as they were concerned. They were an item the moment they met in homeroom the first day of our freshman year. They took the same classes, always sat together during lunchtime, and attended every school dance (where they always won the favorite couple award). Myles proposed to LouEllen on our graduation day in front of the entire student body when he went onstage to receive his diploma. When it was her turn fifteen minutes later — and it had to be the longest fifteen minutes of Myles's life — she sobbed a yes. The entire assembly burst into a thunderous ovation as he returned to the stage, sweeping her up in his arms. As they sealed it with a kiss, the band began to play "Here Comes the Bride." After witnessing such a public display, one could not help but assume that they were meant to be together and that what they had would last forever.

But everyone knew there was trouble in paradise when LouEllen arrived at the reunion first and the man on her arm was not Myles but Jake, her "soon-to-be second husband" (as she introduced him). Myles followed a few minutes later with his current mate — who was also a man! And it didn't help that Donovan, Myles's man, was better looking than Jake (while Donovan had that grunge look going on, Jake just looked *grungy* — and I guess he would, since he manages an auto parts store in Bensonhurst).

Myles and LouEllen avoided each other all evening, declined posing together for a photo for the school's archives, and whenever their breakup was broached, they both brushed it off (not wanting to discuss such personal business was their right, but it was pretty obvious *why* they got a divorce). Donovan, who disclosed that he and Myles had been together for close to three years, let it slip that they were involved in a real family feud, battling for custody of the children, two girls and a boy: Josie, eight; Libby, six; and Parker, four. He showed me a photo of them. I wanted to ask how LouEllen viewed him (not to mention what the children called him), but I guess LouEllen's assertion (as reported by him) that her son doesn't need "three daddies" and that they'd never get their hands on her son and turn him into one of them spelled it out for me. I only hope LouEllen's problem with who her husband is isn't passed on to her kids.

Manuel Gutierrez. Born in Belize but raised in Hell's Kitchen, he was the editor of the school

newspaper, and if he wasn't, I'm sure I would
never have gotten to write half the stories I did
(that exposé on how students have found more
ingenious ways of cheating on tests really sent
the faculty into a tizzy and got me some hate
mail) or publish my own column. Manny (as he
liked to be called) also published a column of
his own on entertainment. I confess to being a
bona fide music junkie, but Manny was a certi-
fiable culture vulture. He read *Billboard*,
Variety, and *The Hollywood Reporter* religious-
ly and vowed that he not only would one day
write for all three but also would name his four
children after the top show-business awards:
Tony, Emmy, Grammy, and Oscar.

Well, after freelancing for *Billboard* during
his college years and interning at *The
Hollywood Reporter*, *Variety* snatched him up.
And although he vowed to stay single through
his twenties (as he once declared, "I want my
twenties to be *roaring*"), he got married after a
two-week romance to Juanita Cordero, an
actress from Madrid he met while attending
(and covering) the Cannes Film Festival last
year. She didn't come to the reunion because
she is pregnant — *very* pregnant. She should be
dropping Tony, Emmy, Grammy, *and* Oscar

any minute. But since she's carrying three girls and a boy, Tony will be a Tonie, and Grammy will be a nickname for Gramiela.

But since he didn't have a photo of his youngsters to show yet, he turned to what he loved to discuss the most: wondering out loud if anyone else in our class predicted that Marisa Tomei would shock the world and win the Supporting Actress Oscar last year or remembered she was also a graduate of our school. I had to admit in both cases that I didn't. Of course, my admission led to his handicapping the race and recalling her other endeavors. I didn't mind his recounting her career, since he was (and still is) nice to look at: He's my height, weight, and skin color, with large gray eyes, thick eyebrows that almost connect above his nose, a short curly 'fro parted near his right temple, and a dimple in his left cheek. He's now sporting glasses, Ray-Bans no doubt, that he says are prescription. The dark frames make him even more sexy.

Demetrius Hightower. His last name didn't suit him, since he was only five feet tall. He was called the Black Tattoo; folks would mimic Herve Villechaize in *Fantasy Island* (remember that show?), pointing upward and shouting

"Da plane, Boss, da plane!" And his going bald at such a young age didn't help him gain any fans either. Some joked that he was really an old man trapped in a little boy's body.

No one was laughing at or making fun of him tonight, though. Totally bald with two small gold hoops in both ears, he looked like a pint-size Pooquie. When he took off his tuxedo jacket, all heads turned (including mine) — and *gasped*. He's twice as big as he was in high school, and his starched white shirt could not hide the brawn. In fact, when he flexed, his biceps expanded and grew so large and high (à la Popeye), it seemed as if that mound of muscle would pop out of his sleeve. The one body par**t** fully exposed was his neck — and he even had muscles there! Every time he moved, those muscles moved right along with him — and so did several of the women jockeying to be on his jock.

One of them was Arnetia Harrison, the snootiest, snobbiest sister in our class. Coming from a family in which the five previous generations had all gone to college, she just knew she was part of an elite class and, hence, was better than anybody else, male or female, Black or white. But she was particularly mean to Demetrius. She would never give him the time

11

of day in high school — and there wasn't a day that went by when he didn't ask to spend some time with her — but her tune most certainly had changed now. She was reaching out and touching — *a lot*. Demetrius was being a little too nice to her: After all, she had been the cause of most of his problems (she usually started that Greek chorus in the halls), and she never had a kind word to say to or about him (in his high school yearbook, she wrote, "I hope you grow — UP!").

But the reason why he was being so gracious appeared a half hour after he arrived. His wife, Ona, another chocolate-drop cutie, is also a bodybuilding champ. In the end, having Arnetia see what she couldn't have — and, in the case of Ona, what she couldn't *be* — was all the satisfaction he needed. Walking away from them somewhat humiliated, Arnetia, I suppose, felt even more embarrassed, considering sixty more minutes of sand had been poured into that hourglass figure she used to have.

Norman Dunne. He was called Norm the Nerd by most, and he looked and acted the role (glasses taped at the bridge, bow ties, beanies, and the ever-important high-water trousers that always fell right above the ankle). But to me he was the Great White Dope. Every time he opened his mouth, it was "A Bicentennial Minute": Give us that poor, that tired, that hud-dled masses nonsense. In his eyes America is and always will be the greatest country on earth and has never done and could never do wrong.

As you've probably guessed, this made us rivals. Things always came to a head in history class. I was taught to question everything I learned in school, especially when it came to how events, issues, and people are recorded and presented. And given how I almost never saw myself or my people recorded and presented in a manner familiar to me, I knew better than to just accept the word of a textbook or teacher (whenever I believed we were being rendered invisible, I would ask, "Where are the Black people?" and follow it up with "I *know* we were there!"). But Norm, just like too many students white *and* Black, readily accepted the idea that Negroes have contributed nothing to society (and how can one not believe this when we first appear as property, are "freed," disappear for a century, and then reappear in the '60s during the civil rights movement?). Since all that we are and have is because of white folks (yeah, right), we should embrace their world and the

way they view it because there is only one way
to view this world, and they are the center of it.

I don't think so.

So you can imagine his shock when I stated
that, while he may view George Washington
and those other DWEMs (dead white European
males) as being *his* Founding Fathers, they certainly aren't *mine;* that, no matter how much
the South may mythologize, the Civil War was
not about "states' rights"; and that Christopher
Columbus could not have "discovered" a land
that had been populated by others (peacefully,
mind you) for thousands of years.

And then there was our sour debate about
slavery and its relevancy today...

"But it doesn't matter anymore, Mitchell."
"I'm sorry?"
"It doesn't matter."
"How can it not matter?"
"It happened a long time ago."
"A hundred years is not a long time ago."
"It's in the past. That's why we are studying
it in a history class."
"So long as there are millions of Black folks
walking around with surnames that don't
belong to them, it's living *history."*

14

Of course, he and the rest of the class gagged (he also gave me *that* shrug and *that* sigh that said, "*Oh*, boy, *there* you go again").

But something must've happened since we last saw each other to make him stop viewing the lives of folks who are not white with indifference: He returned to Edward R. Murrow High School with a wife named Carmela — who is Black.

There was a buzz when they walked in together, since she could pass for Iman (and he, unfortunately, for David Bowie). And like that infamous couple, she definitely stood above him — like, a good five inches (and she wasn't wearing heels!). She is very much a people person, warming up to everyone she met. And she obviously has Norman somewhat in check: During the course of the night, I overheard her tell the "When I met him he was just a white boy, and now he's transcended his race" story a dozen times as he stood off to her side with that "enlightened" look on his face.

But, of course, he still needs counseling. After telling me how they met (she was part of a team of corporate lawyers who represented his computer design firm in a copyright suit), he confided, "You know, Mitchell, I understand you now."

15

I made eye contact with him; yes, he was wearing a different pair of glasses (thank God) that didn't make him look so nerdy. "Excuse me?"

"I understand you now. I know how you feel and why you feel the way you do." He looked at and nodded at his wife. "The way most of you do."

I could have refrained from annihilating him, but I couldn't resist. My reply: "Just because you're sleeping with *one* of us doesn't mean you're sleeping with *all* of us."

He stayed clear of me for the rest of the night.

Stefan "Huey" Gillmore. He was nicknamed Huey because, just like that famous Black Panther, he was all about uplifting his people. He formed the school's Black Student Union (BSU), created an underground one-page newsletter called *The Black Sheet* that served as a platform for his own views about Black empowerment, and discouraged folks from participating in Black History Month celebrations, arguing that "our history deserves to be talked about more than twenty-eight days each year." He even looked the part of a revolutionary: a mushroom-cloud Afro that a pick often sat atop of, dashikis, and cowrie shells, and he carried

around copies of *Soul on Ice* and *Afrocentricity*,
which he would sometimes recite from, depend-
ing on the topic of the moment.

The faculty tolerated his "Black is beautiful"
philosophy; Mr. Leonardo, the principal, even
excused him when he wouldn't recite the Pledge
of Allegiance (in Huey's eyes it was "yet another oppressive symbol of white supremacy"). But
Mr. Leonardo put his foot down when he began
burning incense in the BSU office and refused
to allow whites to attend BSU meetings (facing
suspension, Huey relented on both but made
BSU meetings so uncomfortable for the few
whites who did come, they didn't return). I
always pictured him changing his name (something he said he planned to do when he turned
18) and becoming a disciple of Islam. As it stated in our yearbook, his goal was "to wake my
people up."

What a difference a decade made.

Upon first glance I thought he would be intro-
ducing himself as Brother X, for he had on a
brown suit with a bow tie. But the Afro was
replaced by a glossy, slicked-back hairstyle.
*Hmm...there's no way he could be in the Nation
with a conk*, I thought to myself as we shook
hands. And he isn't: He's an ordained evangelical

minister. And where did he study? Regent University, the religious school founded by Pat Robertson. And not only is he a member of the Christian Coalition, he is also, as his business card announced, a "Minority Outreach Coordinator & Family Values Advocate" (uh-huh...he helps Ralph Reed, who reminds me of a Gestapo security officer, to spread the Gospel of Hate about homosexuals in communities of color).

He explained that his transformation into a foot soldier for the Lord happened after he dropped out of Howard University and found himself a homeless drug addict. A "missionary" from the Coalition approached him one day on the street and persuaded him to attend a church service (after which he was promised a hot meal and a bed for the night), and it was there that he was born again and accepted his new calling. He married that woman who, as he put it, "saved my life"; he produced a photo of her (to my surprise, she was Black, leading me to believe that *they* must have been the two Negroes shown during the Republican National Convention telecast two years ago). When I asked whether the liberation of Black folks was no longer a worthy cause, he said, "I am fighting for the liberation of *all* my people, regardless of color. No cause is greater than saving souls for *Him*."

And following this declaration, he called himself trying to save *my* soul and the souls of others in the room. I brushed off his "Do you know God?" queries and crushed his attempts to get me to join his ministry in Plainfield, New Jersey. But he got me all fired up when he proceeded to insult Myles and Donovan — as well as Angela Martin, a sister from our class whose coochie he was always trying to bang (now he knew why he couldn't), and her partner, Eunique — as each couple jammed off Daryl Hall and John Oates's "Maneater."

He shook his head, visibly disturbed. "Can you *believe* that? It is a disgrace! It is an affront to all that is good and decent! It is an abomination in God's eyes!"

Yeah, I let him have it. "How do *you* know? Do you have Jesus' fax number?" With his mouth agape, I politely excused myself.

And he, like Norm, avoided me for the remainder of the evening.

Lily Hashawahara. Her mother was only three when she became one of the 110,000 Japanese-Americans forced to live in detention camps after Japan bombed Pearl Harbor and dragged the U.S. into World War II. But in spite of that demoralizing, tragic event, her mother encouraged her to hold dear the principles of America: life, liberty, and the pursuit of happiness. In addition to being president of the student body and chair of the student council, Lily was my academic rival, finishing either a point ahead of or behind me in grade-point-average rankings each semester. When graduation day arrived I was in the "win" position; she, in "place" (Norm had to settle for the "show" slot). We received an equal number of medals (seven) and plaques from the Honor Society and were both expected to conquer the fields we expressed interest in (she, business; myself, journalism).

But her quest to achieve the American dream went, as Pooquie would say, *wack:* She returned with Bette Davis's eyes, Julia Roberts's cheeks, and Carly Simon's lips. She let it slip several times that, as a vice president at Dean Witter, she was one of the youngest executives and the highest ranking ethnic minority at the organization (the way she looks, it's no wonder). One thing, though, *hadn't* changed: She still cackles like a hen, and I overheard more than one person crack, "Is she ever going to lay that egg?"

LaDonna Ciccone. She smacked gum and blew bubbles bigger than her face, painted her nails every day during lunch, drank milk and Coke (Laverne De Fazio's concoction wasn't sweet enough for her), and wore a button with a profile of Deney Terrio, the host of the music TV series *Dance Fever,* pinned to her chest the entire four years ("I'm gonna marry that man one day," she'd often coo). She also claimed that the similarity between her name and that of a singer whose star was quickly rising was not a coincidence (I don't know if she's related to Madonna, but like the Material Girl, she top-knotted her hair and occasionally donned crucifix earrings). LaDonna didn't want to dance in music videos or on television, though: She wanted to kick up her heels as a Rockette.

That didn't happen, but something extraordinary did: She won the Publishers Clearing House Sweepstakes four years ago. She was captured on film — head wrapped up in yellow rollers, screaming and crying uncontrollably — as she was presented with a check for $400,000. A small sum, yes, but a piece of change nice enough that she could "retire" (figuratively speaking, of course, since she was unemployed at the time). She, her teenage brother, and her mother moved out of the two-bedroom apartment they shared in Howard Beach, Queens, and into a three-bedroom home in Hicksville, a 'burb out on Long Island. She also opened up a hair salon in the old neighborhood called LaDonna's Boudoir of Beauty.

But we were able to see for ourselves where the money was going: Besides the snakeskin jacket and boots, the glad-rag blouse, the Tarlazzi skirt, and the "blowout" perm (the hair was *everywhere*), there were (as the Children would put it) the *breasts-uh-sis*, which had gone from a B cup to a D cup (yeah, she blabbed). Her bust was definitely a bust now, and many of the men (as well as a few women) in the room leered at her oversize bowling pins with lust. It was, quite frankly, a miracle she could *walk* with them: She's only a few inches taller than Demetrius.

Hunt Grecco. Besides being president of the Greek Club and having a very bad case of halitosis, this one was just cuckoo for cocoa cock. For him, any old Black would do. He'd lurk in the locker room and showers, just itchin' to see somethin' swingin' (I caught him a few times tryin' to peep me). He was into us before we were *in*, and now that we are, I'm sure he's got a lot of competition from our other "admirers" of the Caucasian persuasion.

But I know he hasn't been wantin' over the past few years because I've been *seeing* all the dick he's been getting. He's an actor, but a very special kind — the kind that can take twelve inches without a flinch. He's one of the regulars featured in these interracial videos put out by a triple-X film company called Ebony on Ivory. The titles say it all: *The Halfblack of Notre Dame*; *Vanilla Fudged*; *Blacks & Blues*; *Black Where I Started From*; *The Honky N the 'Hood*; and *Blacked Out*.

I've had the pleasure of seeing only one of his performances: An ex happened to have a copy of *Till Dick Do Us Part*, claiming it was one of his favorite fuck films. Well, it didn't become one of mine. In it Hunt (the name suits him in both real life *and* reel life) plays a waiter at a wedding reception who ends up truly serving the groom, his younger brother, his best man, the caterer, even the father of the bride in a bathroom, the kitchen, a walk-in closet, and a limousine. I wanted so bad to ask about his adventures in the land of porn but decided not to burst his bubble. If he wanted folks to believe he was a stuntman in Hollywood (and he'd have to be to do some of the things *he's* done on film), I was willing to go along.

Candyce "Candy" Lane. She was crazy about Stacy Lattisaw and even favored her a bit. She wore that cornrow 'do that white folks *still* believe Bo Derek invented, and just about everything in her wardrobe was made by those two famous sisters — Poly and Ester. And, yeah, girlfriend loved to eat candy — and ingesting all that artificial flavoring and coloring obviously went straight to her head. She was sillier than one of my best friends, B.D., the original Brain Dense. How dense was she? Well, if Candy took the Pepsi challenge, she would've chosen Dr Pepper.

But it's the dense ones that you have to watch out for. She's probably the last person any of us thought would end up being a millionaire, but she is. How did she do it? Well, when she was a showgirl in Las Vegas several years ago, she visited one of her beaus in Austin, Texas, who decided that the perfect place to take her to experience real Southwestern comfort was a restaurant called Hooters. Yes, *that* Hooters. She became angry — but not because the women were half dressed, flaunting and flailing their physiques to earn a living. She thought it was unfair that women didn't have such an establishment. So she borrowed $50,000 from a bank and opened up Hoofers, a restaurant where the waiters, busboys, and even the hosts walk around in boxer shorts and tanks. Five years later there are now a dozen Hoofers restaurants in Texas. And after the success of a gay version in San Francisco and an all-Black version in Atlanta, she's planning to open up two in New York this fall: one in Chelsea, the other in Harlem (I plan to be at the ground-breaking ceremony for the latter).

Still deliriously sweet and silly, she truly looked like the millionairess she is: A black short-sleeved, bell-bottomed, see-through silk pantsuit (similar to Babs's fashion shocker at the 1968 Academy Awards) showed off her slinky showgirl shape, and those glamorous short spiral curls couldn't hide her ears, which were adorned with the biggest pair of karats I'd ever seen. Uh-huh, no more Poly or Ester for *this* sister.

Troy Fauntleroy. Unsatisfied with the High School for the Performing Arts ("Everybody is a star there, and I want to be the *only* one"), he transferred to Murrow as a junior and did a serious diva turn when he was offered the role of Leading Player in *Pippin*. He wanted to play Pippin. Of course, the faculty balked; they tried to convince him that he was "born to portray Leading Player," arguing that Ben Vereen won a Tony when it was on Broadway. But Troy had them to know that (1) he wasn't Ben Vereen, (2) this ain't Broadway, and (3) he wasn't playin' second fiddle to some white boy — especially when he could sing, dance, *and* act better than the person they chose to play Pippin, Kip Canady (while Troy wasn't the least bit modest about his talent, *that* observation was certainly true: The only thing Kip had goin' for him were those Montgomery Clift looks, for he couldn't carry a tune, was pigeon-toed, and had trouble remembering his class schedule, so how would he be able to memorize the lead in a musical?).

The theater staff, though, were adamant about the casting and just knew that Troy would accept "his place" (as one of those fools stated). But Troy made them gag: With Huey's help he organized a protest outside the school. He and his troupe, carrying signs that read COLOR-BLIND CASTING OR BLIND CASTING? and CURTAINS FOR BLACK ACTORS, managed to raise enough noise to get on the 6 o'clock news.

And Troy did his homework: He discovered that the school had done only one production in its ten-year history that actually afforded Black and other students of color the opportunity to perform: *West Side Story*. Yet even in this case the school hypocritically practiced its own form of racist typecasting: They had no problem with all the knife-wielding Sharks and their spitfire girlfriends being portrayed by members of the Latino student body (which basically meant *every* Latino student in the school) but insisted that, as was the case with the original stage version and the film, Maria be played by someone white (and let it be stated that, according to the school paper's then-critic, that "white" Maria, Greta Van Hausen — who in her stage debut as Blanche DuBois turned *A Streetcar Named Desire* into *A Streetcar Named Disaster* — possessed neither the dramatic range of Carol Lawrence nor the movie-star sensuality of Natalie Wood).

So with history on his side and a look of amused condescension on his face that screamed "See, I *told* you so," Troy peered into the TV cameras and uttered an unforgettable ten-second sound bite: "If Louis Gossett Jr. can play a role not written for a Black actor in *An*

Officer and a Gentleman, I can certainly do the same in a high school production."

A spokeswoman for the Negro Ensemble Company, a local theater group, agreed: "Who would ever think that, at a high school specifically created to build bridges, such a blatant act of discrimination would take place?" As you can imagine, the board of education was not the least bit pleased with the negative publicity surrounding what one official called "such a trivial matter," and after they called an emergency meeting with Mr. Leonardo, Troy got the part.

Yes, he was great as Pippin — and the Most Happy Fella and Jesus Christ Superstar. And, yes, Troy should have been a Broadway star. But Hinton Battle beat him to the punch. You know the rules: Only one of us can be on top at once. That's why Alfonso Ribeiro got wise and tap-danced his way onto *The Fresh Prince of Bel Air* (he knew them offers would *not* be comin'). After graduating from Yale's drama program, Troy found himself in road productions of *Ain't Misbehavin'* and *Sophisticated Ladies* but realized this wasn't where his *true* talent lay. So he got into the promotion end and is now one of only a few Black agents in the theater (according to him, you can count them all on *three* fingers). But he's much happier knowing he's getting a steady paycheck and isn't out on the road fifty weeks out of a year. Most of his clients are white men, an irony that isn't lost on him ("It's about time *they* sweat to make one of *us* a dollar, you know?"). He's still got that great bod, and judging from the moves he displayed on the dance floor, he's still got *it*, but I'm sure he wouldn't be getting much work, given the nose ring and his cherries jubilee hair.

Now, while I knew all these people, I didn't *know* them. I recognized them by reputation, and our conversations revolved around the myths and legacies attached to their names. I couldn't call any of them friends; they were barely acquaintances. I didn't really have friends in high school; I guess I was a loner. I never warmed up to being a part of a clique, and that seemed to be what high school was all about: trying to find something, some*one* to belong to, that will help you find and define yourself.

I did, though, get to experience this in a way that some, I'm sure, would be disgusted or disturbed by. But it was only after I had made my rounds of the entire hall (it was actually the first-floor gym immaculately decorated as a ballroom), exhausting the phrases "Is that really you?" "You look fabulous," and "It's great to see you" (as well as my cheekbones, which were tight from all that smiling), that I would relive that time.

I decided to take a break and make myself invisible by standing against the wall near the back of the hall, away from the crowds, away from the commotion, and away from the lights. I sipped on some champagne and listened as the twenty-second consecutive song by a white artist — "Love Is a Battlefield" by Pat Benatar — played (I'm quite sure that Black folks produced some sort of music worthy to be listened to between the years 1980 and 1984, but I didn't plan on being around at the end of the evening, when I knew we would finally be acknowledged). Given that this was the fourth straight tune about the hard knocks one suffers being in love (the other three being Neil Diamond's "Love on the Rocks," Juice Newton's "Love's Been a Little Bit Hard on Me" and Culture Club's "Do You Really Want to Hurt Me?" — it was only fitting that, at that moment, when I decided to have a seat at a table nearby, I would hear *his* voice.

"Ah…don't get comfortable."

I — or, rather, my behind — stopped. My body rose, and I stood erect. I didn't have to turn around to see who it was; I had been waiting all night to hear that voice. He was the reason I came tonight. He was the person I wished to see.

Just hearing that voice...

Just hearing those words...

Those same words...

It was just like...the first time.

The First Time We Met...

...it was the last period on the first day of my junior year, and it felt like I had roughed the entire semester.

Just another forty-five minutes and it would all be over. This is what I get, going to a magnet school: you know, those educational institutions created to promote "integration" — meaning that the school's student population must always be half white and that only a handful of the faculty is of color. The message: that going to school with and being taught by whites is going to make us "disadvantaged" minority kids better students and, later in life, better people. *Puh-leeze.* I've come across more idiots in this school, both students and faculty, than I ever did attending predominantly Black schools in Bed-Stuy.

But because the white-is-right theory drives the system, Murrow High is one of the most well-equipped, spacious schools in the city. It's a bright red brick building with five floors, covering what amounts to one city block. The grounds are kept up — no litter on the streets, sidewalks, or varsity field's artificial turf. There is no graffiti on the walls inside or outside the building (and don't even let them catch you with a spray can — your ass is suspended for a week). There are no overcrowded classrooms (the average class size is twenty-four) and enough textbooks to go around. There's even a TV studio, a mini-planetarium, and a computer room, things one would never see in a neighborhood like mine.

But one has to pay a price for going to a school like this (uh-huh, ain't nothin' in this life free). Since attending such a school is viewed as an "experiment," everybody is watching you, from your parents to the board of ed to the mayor. We, the students, are supposed to set a standard for educational excellence and racial/ethnic/cultural/religious tolerance that the rest of our peers in the city (and the nation) can follow. As a result, any new programs or policies they want to try, they try on us — after all, we're also supposed to be mature enough to handle it. So while the rest of the city's students are already home or hanging out with their friends, my 2,400 schoolmates and I actually attend classes (I'd love to know what board of ed bureaucrat thought *this* unbrilliant idea up). The teachers don't assign homework, but attendance is taken, and we engage in either a teenage version of "What I did during my summer vacation" ("Anyone go anywhere or do anything extraordinary?") or talk about what the teacher expects from us and what we expect from the class (as if one expects to get *anything* out of calculus).

At least with calculus and the other academic courses, I knew I would be challenged. But I was in phys ed class — a "course" that did not stimulate me in the least. To say that I didn't like it would be putting it mildly. I absolutely *hated* it. I never cared for it, ever since elementary school. What can I say? I just wasn't the sports-playing type.

And while I don't think my distaste for athletics had anything to do with my being gay, I do know that being gay made me self-conscious about not making myself *look* like I was. In other words, because balls of any stripe, size, or shape did not mesh or match well with my hands, I avoided all contact with them ingeniously during my first two years at Murrow. When we had to play baseball, I was the catcher (how could I miss, when the pitcher was aiming straight for my glove?). When we had to play football, I submitted a letter to my teacher with a forged signature, explaining that I could not partake in rough play. With basketball I had help being invisible: I managed to play on teams where the other players knew not to trust me with the ball (every team I was on won, with no help from me). The only two activities I participated in where the ball actually touched my bare hand or palm were volleyball and dodgeball, two games that, as my sarcastic cousin Calvin observed, "any dummy can play."

But as a junior, I was finally out of the danger zone. Upperclassmen (and women) got to choose the sports they wished to participate in. Naturally I went for the easy one: track and field. There was a brief introduction to it during my freshman year. At first it all seemed odd to me — what does running around a field have to do with fitness? But once I learned all about cardiovascular fitness and how the heart, muscles, and lungs are helped by it, I started to enjoy it. So I couldn't wait to sign up for it. But to my dismay Mr. Pulaski's section was all filled up. I had to settle for the only other sport on the list where I felt safe: gymnastics. Of course, I didn't know a thing about cartwheels or parallel bars, but I was willing to try anything but a sport that had a name which ended in *ball.*

The other students in the class seemed to know something about it. Some had slipped off their sneakers to practice their moves and clown around on the equipment. Standing against the wall in the back of the gymnasium, I had a perfect view of the entire room and finally noticed a few things: (1) half the class must have seen *E.T.,* because they were wearing T-shirts with that ugly little alien's face on them; (2) out of forty students, I was one of four males (this didn't bother me: For some reason I was a lot more comfortable with the idea of being seen as a wimp by girls than boys); and (3) I was the lone Black student. Well, isn't *this* great: It's bad enough I have to be "the only one" in my English and history AP (advanced placement) classes. Will I also have to be a credit to my race in an area I have absolutely no interest in?

Not the least bit thrilled with this revelation, I proceeded to flop down on the thick green mat, which covered every inch of the gymnasium floor. My palms were planted and my behind was but one inch from landing when...

"Uh, don't get comfortable."

My body stopped in its squatting position; just my head turned left, in the direction the voice came from. It was deep and dreamy; it rumbled...*softly*. My eyes met not a pair of eyes but knees. They weren't knobby or ashy or scraped. They were, miraculously, the exact same color as the legs they were attached to. *And the legs!* They didn't look real — you know, they were so polished, so...so *perfect*, one would assume they belonged to a mannequin or a G.I. Joe doll with a light caramel tan.

But this wasn't a mannequin. And this G.I. Joe — he just happened to be wearing a pair of camouflage shorts and a black ARMY T-shirt — *was* real.

As I stood up, I looked up...and up...and up. God, how tall *was* this man? After my eyes took in those massive arms, those truck-stop shoulders, that quarterback-jack neck, those chipmunk cheeks, those sparse yet thick lips, and that flat, dignified nose, I finally saw his eyes.

They were dark brown with a hint of green speckled in for added effect — and what an effect they were having on me! I just stood there, frozen. I felt like Diana Ross in *Lady Sings the Blues*, getting a very first look at Billy Dee Williams.

Mmm-hmm. Them there eyes.

"I'm about to begin class. Why don't you come on over?" He nodded toward the other side of the gym and winked. He looked me over once. He grinned. He walked off.

I tried to move but couldn't. I looked down at my paralyzed feet. Uh-oh…I guess I showed him just how much I wanted to come on over. But did he see *it*? I was gasping.

I did my best to cover up my hard-on by holding my knapsack in front of me. I followed him, enjoying the view of his back from the back. And Lord, did *he* have *back!*

He blew a whistle, which was attached to what appeared to be a long, thin red licorice stick that was tied around his neck. "Okay, ladies and gen-tlemen, could you all please take a seat?"

I made my way around him and sat down, crossing my legs and shifting my jeans so that *it* was hidden. I was on his left and now had a great side view (well, it really didn't matter the angle...the view would always be great from any and every angle, slope, and point). I began taking him in from his naked toe (what lovely feet!), when my eyes stopped smack-dab at his middle: That *wasn't* a sock in his crotch. My throat became dry, and my mouth began to water.

He smiled. "I know you've all had a very long day, so we'll keep this as short as possible. I'm Warren Reid, and I'll be your instructor for this gymnastics section."

Hmm...he didn't say "teacher." He didn't say "coach." He said "instructor." Sounds sexy.

"I see a lot of familiar faces...and I also see a few new ones."

He glanced at me with that last statement.

"I'll take attendance and brief you all on what to expect — and I do mean *brief* you. When I call your name, please raise your hand."

He read the roll. I took a deep breath.

"Abernathy."

"Archer."

"Ayala."

"Bailey."

There go the A's. *Exhale. Inhale.*

"Becton."

"Bugliosi."

"Carlyle."

Uh-oh, here come the C's — and there goes my heart, racing out of control.

"Costello."

"Cr—"

I closed my eyes. I prayed it wouldn't be me.

"—anshaw."

Whew, I whispered to myself. I put my hand on my heart. I wasn't ready to be called just then. But I had no choice the next time around.

"Crawford." He smiled, looking at me through the corner of his eye. Hmm...did he know it was me?

I smiled too. I raised my hand.

He checked me off and then checked me out again. With his eyebrows raised, he pointed his pen at me. "Uh, any relation to Randy?"

The man wanted to hold a conversation with me! Yeah, I felt special — none of the other students were queried in such a way.

I folded my hands, dropped them on my legs, and leaned forward as if he were sitting across from me, not standing a few feet away. "Randy? Uh, is he a student at the school?" I asked.

He snickered. "No, no relation."

I was disappointed that it ended as soon as it began. I didn't care that there were thirty other

students waiting to be checked off. And I didn't
get the joke at the time — I didn't know who
Randy Crawford was — but the grin I received
each time our eyes met for the remainder of
that period told me that I *would*.

Mmm-hmm...I had the feeling I was gonna
like this class.

The First Time He Touched Me...

...I literally did a cartwheel.

Have you ever had a crush on a teacher? I'm sure we all have. From the first day, the first moment you meet them, you're...

Captivated.

Captured.

Committed.

Convicted.

My very first crush was on an English teacher named Mr. Weatherspoon in the second grade. He was fresh out of college and looked so fresh (uh, young) that, after meeting him on parent-teacher conference night, my mother just knew she was on *Candid Camera:* She thought he was a student masquerading as a teacher. He just took her observation as a compliment and flashed that smile. Lord, that *smile*. He had what you would call a baby-grand grin. Whenever he flashed it, I would hear them ivories *and* ebonies being tickled (notice how most forget to mention those black keys). And I don't know *what* tune was being played, but whatever it was, it was hypnotic — just like him. He always came to class dressed down in a shirt, jacket, slacks, and tie, and his scent was an aftershave lotion called Blue Musk (yes, I had the gall to ask; there was a reporter in me at that age).

I looked forward to when he would hunch over my desk, give me one of those smiles, reach out with that big, brown hand, and crown me the winner of our weekly spelling bee by brushing my head and saying, "*Out*standing, Mitchell. Just outstanding." And I *earned* that reward every week: I studied an extra hour each Thursday afternoon to ensure that I held on to my title. When he smiled at me, when he touched me...I don't know, *that* button was pressed. Yeah, it was an innocent gesture and in no way sexual, but it had the opposite effect: Those homohormones really kicked into gear. I didn't know at that age what it was I was feeling or why I was feeling the way I was, but I knew that I *loved* the feeling.

But I was fully aware of what I was feeling and *why* I was feeling it this time. And I was truly enjoying what those homohormones were doing to me. I was in a daze, a haze over Mr. Reid: I just stared into space in all my classes, daydreaming about him. And at night? My wet dreams were so wild that I found my pillow and sheet on the floor in the morning and my underwear soaked. In a sense I had my art teacher, Ms. Yearwood, to thank for that. I dreamed of Mr. Reid totally naked, glossed in oil, posing as if he were Michelangelo's *David*. Naturally I wanted to do more than just dream about him, night or day, naked — and secretly hoped that he did too.

I have always believed that everything happens for a reason, that people come in and out of your life for a purpose. So I just knew that our finally· meeting was fate, a happening that was supposed to be. How else can one explain our being in the same school five days a week for two years and never having a class together, never even *seeing* each other in the hallway? Well, maybe he had seen me before, but I didn't know he existed. I didn't think there were any Black male teachers

at the school. There was only one female: Ms.
Dawson, who was, for lack of a better phrase, the
mammy of the place: a short, stout woman who
was one grit away from being on a box of pan-
cakes. She was definitely a "good Negress": She
cheesed it up so much, it turned my stomach. To
think that Mr. Reid had been here all this time,
and I didn't know…? Yeah, I felt cheated.

And yeah, I wanted to make up for lost time.

So, as you can imagine, I had never been so
eager to get to gym class. I raced from my
Spanish class on the first floor to the locker
rooms on the second, changed into my shorts
and T-shirt, and was on the third-floor gymnasium in a record six minutes. I was usually the
very last person to make my entrance (no, I was
never in a hurry to get there), but today — and
every day thereafter — I was the first. I stood in
the spot we first met, hoping he would reenter
my life through the same doors he came
through. The door opened two dozen times —
and every single time, a white face or faces
came through (no, I was not pleased). Then…

"All right, folks, let me have your attention,
please."

He emerged from the other side of the gym.
Damn! I didn't want anyone to see him before I

did (how about that: I was already being pos-
sessive when he wasn't mine to possess). As I
made my way toward him, I gasped when he
was finally in full view. He had on a gray sweat
tank and pants. Such an outfit clings to *everything* — and boy, oh, boy, did it cling to Mr.
Reid. He filled *in* that outfit, and I would love
to have been there when he poured his body
into it.

"We have a lot to do today, so I just want to
take attendance quick. As I call you, count off
and create eight rows, five people in each row,
back to front. These will be your assigned
places for the semester."

When he got to me, I ended up being first in
the second row. You know I was just too happy.
I had a ringside seat to watch him exert every
part of his body. Just thinking about it was
making me hot.

He finished attendance, bent his body forward,
and placed his clipboard on the floor, but his
body was curled, as if he were doing a curtsy.

Good God, what grace.

"Now, we're going to do a basic exercise routine. This will be the warm-up you will warm up
with every day. But in order to exercise right,
you have to *breathe* right. Notice how when

most people inhale, their stomach goes in." He demonstrated, but I didn't see anything go in. "Well, that's *not* the way to breathe. When you inhale, your stomach is supposed to come *out*..." He attempted to show us this too, but I didn't see his stomach move outward. It was clear that he didn't *have* a stomach. The only thing pushing out was his chest. His shirt lifted along with it, outlining those curves even more.

Mercy.

We practiced inhaling and exhaling for a bit and then got to the warm-up. Now, the exercises were basic — jumping jacks, sit-ups, leg lifts, even jogging in place. But I wasn't taking a chance in this area: I prepared by practicing these and other basics at home. Being the only Black male in the class, I knew that I was expected to have all the right moves — I didn't have the luxury of looking like Goldie Hawn in *Private Benjamin,* barely able to do a push-up. But, of course, I really wanted to impress my instructor — and I did. While he complimented me twice on my stance and execution, he lovingly criticized several others, becoming somewhat flustered at one point and declaring, "You folks can't be *that* rusty after two months. You should be able to do these exercises in your sleep."

I was pumped up after the workout but not because of the workout itself: I worked up a sweat watching *him* work up a sweat. Instead of paying attention to my own moves, I kept my eyes on his. I could feel his every bend, his every crunch, his every reach, his every thrust. After he had us shake out the kinks (and, yes, I zeroed in on that bulge, which was shakin' quite nicely), he began the lecture.

"There are four things you need in gymnastics: balance, flexibility, strength, and spatial awareness. They will help you plot and perform to the best of your ability." And he proceeded to test us on all four with the trampoline. This scared me to death. I've always been afraid of heights. I can remember crying my eyes out on class trips to the Statue of Liberty and the Empire State Building. I was afraid I would fall over the railing or out the window and that the whole structure would come tumbling down on top of me. So I didn't look forward to tramping on the trampoline, even if Mr. Reid was helping and guiding us through. I decided I would be last so that I could study the others and not make the same mistakes they did. As he gave us pointers on technique and control, I made my way to the back of the crowd.

When my turn came I was less tense, and whatever fear I had disappeared as soon as he took my hand. Even though it had been touched up with the sweat of thirty-nine other students, it was dry yet smooth. He gripped my hand; his swallowed mine. Our flesh molded, smoldered, as the electricity traveled up my arm and into the rest of my body.

I was still a little apprehensive, but he calmed the fear, looking deep into my eyes. "Don't worry. You'll do fine." He smiled.

I smiled back, climbed up, positioned myself in the middle, and started to jump. I kept my eyes on him, making sure he knew that every move I made depended on him. If he said to land on my knees, I did. If he said to land on the right side of my rump, I did. If he said to land on my back, I did. If he said to do a split or flip in the air — things no one else was asked to do — I did. It was easier than I thought it would be but only because I, as Mr. Reid observed, remembered the instructions: Keep your balance, stay loose, rely on your body weight, and be aware of where you start, where you have to go, and where you have to finish. Oh, and don't forget to *breathe* correctly. Yeah, I really impressed the instructor this time.

"Great form, Crawford, great form!" he praised.

As I came off the trampoline, to the applause and shouts of some, he helped me as he did the other students. But unlike what he did with the others, when my feet landed on the ground, his big brown hand landed on and completely covered my butt.

My knees knocked — and locked. And I *gasped*.

"Now that Mr. Crawford has given us such a splendid routine on the tramp, we'll see if he can repeat this on the mat," he announced as his hand traveled *slowly* up my back and he ushered me over to the middle of the gym.

At that moment I experienced what they would call a chill up my spine. And I *gawked*.

"All right. Now we're going to do one of the elementary movements in gymnastics: the cartwheel."

Uh-oh...another frightful flashback came back to haunt me: my younger brother, Adam, attempting this in our very compact bedroom, hitting his head on the edge of a desk and ending up with fourteen stitches. While the chances of that actually happening to me were slim — there was nothing but space around me — I wasn't so sure I would be able to live up to Mr. Reid's expectations.

But he was.

Once again he demonstrated, movement for movement, and did a few for us. *Ah*...the way he stood, the way his whole body folded and followed his lead, springing up and into the air, the way his hands palmed the mat, the way he brought it on home. Even the way his toes pointed toward the ceiling...yes, it turned me the *fuck* on. I was enjoying him so much that I forgot I was next.

He stood behind me. He took me by the waist — his palms were rather warm, and that warmed me up — and pushed forward into me with *that*. We had never been this close, and no man had ever been this *up* close and personal with me before. *It* was hard and...was it my imagination, or does it not like what it is brushing up against? My dick got happy too, and I was lovin' this press and mesh so much that he had to tell me to assume the position — i.e., throw my hands in the air and spread 'em, along with my legs — three times before I heard him (yes, it's a position I would be in many, many, *many* times).

"All right, slant..."

He slanted along with me.

"…spring, *up*…"

He gave me a little push as he let go of my waist but stood by. Good thing my shirt was tucked inside my pants — it would've blocked my view. Standing on my hands, I got a different view of him — and he was a fine specimen upside down too.

"…and *over*, and *down*."

With his arms out to catch me if I fell, I completed the cartwheel, landing in the position I started in.

"Very good, Crawford. Now let's see if you can do it by yourself."

Yeah, this was the ultimate test. I walked back to where it all began. I assumed the position. I drew back (or, rather, out) a breath.

Slant.

Spring.

Up.

Over.

Down.

Done.

"Really, *really* good, Crawford. Okay. Let's see if your classmates can wheel it like you."

Only a few could come close, and they had taken the class before. I was proud of myself.

But I was even more proud that I had made *him* proud. During the rest of that period, when we would happen to glance each other's way and make eye contact, *that* nod, *that* wink, or *that* smile, gestures I knew were meant only for me, said it all. And it made me wonder...

Where have you been all my life?

The First Time He Held Me...

...I learned to relax, relate, and release *years before Debbie Allen gave the same advice to Jasmine Guy on* A Different World.

After my first day on the mat, Mr. Reid officially made me his "point man" — i.e., he would present every new exercise and introduce our prospective movements on the equipment using *my* body. This meant that while I was lifting and lunging, he'd be spotting and spurring me on, grasping and gripping me *all* over: the balls of my feet, my ankles, my calves, my knees, my thighs, my waist, my belly, my chest (my nipples would perk and protrude), my elbows, my arms, my armpits (which tickled and made me giggle), my back, my neck, my hands (uh, could you, like, never let me go?), and, yes, my ass (cup it, cop it, and co-*opt* it, why don'tcha!). In a way it was torture: It was like we were engaged in foreplay for roughly an hour, and just when it seemed as if he had hit *that* spot again…well, the bell rang. It made me want to resign from my position unless he was willing to take it to the next level. I mean, I was tired of trying to re-create the moves he made on me later that night as I "beat" my way to ecstasy.

But I got over it.

In addition to my being the "teacher's pet," Mr. Reid also decided that I was worthy of being trained. Naturally, this made me pause: *Me? A gymnast?* I think that even *he* knew how absurd his suggestion was — after all, folks became pro basketball/football/baseball celebs. Hell, one could even be a worldwide tennis or racquetball champ. And just the idea of me going for the gold in *any* sport made me — as well as Adam; Anderson, my soon-to-be-stepfather; and Calvin and his twin brother, Alvin — laugh. But Mr. Reid's even suggesting that I had the potential to be an athlete, a contender of *any* kind, pushed me to at least consider challenging my mind *and* my body…for a change.

Thanks to him I was feeling less awkward about my body. I was slim and somewhat trim (not an ounce of baby or teen fat on me), yet I was nothing special to look at (as Tyler Caldwell, our resident high school bully once remarked, "Crawford, you weigh less than a wet noodle"). I guess most would've viewed the state-of-the-art facilities installed in the three gymnasiums in our school as their ticket to a better body and greater self-esteem, but I just sleepwalked through phys ed, going through the motions just to pass my classes. I believed there was no hope for this body I was in, so why even try?

And because I took so little interest in my physical state, my body posture was sluggish. While I didn't sit slumped in chairs or walk with a swagger (the "B-boy bop" was just beginning to emerge), I still had the very bad habits of dragging my feet as I walked and not standing up straight. But that was beginning to change; even my mother remarked how she didn't hear me when I got up for school and passed her bedroom because I was actually picking up my feet when I walked and said she no longer believed that I was born with droopy shoulders.

So as silly and as outrageous as Mr. Reid's invitation was, I accepted it — especially since I'd be practicing an extra hour three days a week after school. We'd have the gym all to ourselves — we'd finally be alone. It was sometimes hard for me to concentrate on what we were there for, and it always depended on what he was *not* wearing. Immediately after class let out, he'd strip off his sweats and give me that *one-on-one* in just his shorts. Watching him contract, contrast, and make contact with almost every arc and arch of that tower of power made me want to contract, contrast, and make contact with him — *and* myself.

Yup, I finally got to know my own body. "*Get* in touch, *stay* in touch, and *touch* your body" was one of Mr. Reid's credos. "You have to *know* your body to *work* your body."

Ain't it the truth.

I got to know all of me — every muscle, every reflex, every joint, every limb — and put each and every one to the test. What a sensual and satisfying journey this was: I never thought my little body was capable of so much...*feeling*. So much...*healing*. And it *was* like a healing, discovering another me, another person *inside* of me. It wasn't a rebirth but a *new* birth.

Whenever I touched myself, I was discovering something new, *becoming* someone new.

And he showed me how to get physical by *getting* physical. He would be the "equipment," and I would "practice" on him. We did some scandalous things, such as standing back-to-back, reaching around the other to clutch the other's waist (I always had to be careful that I wasn't clutching something else). Or there was what I called our "love dance": As he bent down, I'd climb atop his back, jump off onto the ground, and then leap back in the air into his outstretched arms as if he were Alvin Ailey and I were Katherine Dunham.

"All right, Crawford, let me hear your body talk," he would often say as Miss Olivia Neutron-Bomb repeated his command on the stereo. "Let me *hear* it."

I let him hear it — and he liked what he heard.

All this touching and getting in touch with myself did not go unnoticed by my family. Adam wasn't, for the most part, bothered; his only concern was that I was spending too much time on the floor of our room "doing that yoga stuff" and he couldn't practice his jump shot with the makeshift basket he created out of a wire hanger, which was hanging on our closet door (his "ball" was usually a smelly pair of balled-up socks).

My mother was a little skeptical at first — she just knew I couldn't be her elder son, opting to go outside and stretch those legs instead of staying in and reading a good book. She nearly fainted when I requested my own dumbbell set for Christmas (I didn't want to share my brother's, which in the past I would pick up only if he had left them on my bed). And she became worried when I began meditating. No, I didn't chant as if I were a Buddhist, but I did sometimes hum and "call out" (*to* what and *for* what, I don't really know). Mr. Reid said that this would put me in the right frame of mind and help me make that spiritual connection inside, clearing any and all negativity so that I could *relax, relate, and release* to all of me (and it did).

Anderson thought he had my transformation into a high school jock figured out: "He must be trying to impress *somebody* at that school. He must have a crush on a young lady."

Well, he got it half right.

Crush or no crush, my mother still wasn't keen about my getting too serious about gymnastics. She felt my plate was already full — taking the

AP classes, writing a column for the school paper, studying for the SAT — and that it was kind of late in the game for me to be getting *into* the game. But Anderson sweet-talked her into it, even though he didn't quite view gymnastics as a real sport ("Yeah, you gettin' some exercise, but I bet you don't *really* sweat").

Well, I put her fears to rest and forced him to reconsider any doubts he had about my "sweatability" when a community-wide competition was held the weekend before Thanksgiving. The top five seeds would go on to the citywide finals in January. When the final scores were tallied and I won, I screamed and squealed with delight as Mr. Reid threw me up in the air and twirled us around.

And then, for one and *only* one second, my arms settled around his neck, his arms tightened around my waist, our eyes met, and...

BAM!

Now, he had "held" me many times before, and it was usually on the rebound, the inbound, the outbound, the upbound, the downbound, the overbound, the underbound, or the endbound (yeah, we got around the bound). But this time it was...*different*. We both knew it, we both saw it, we both *felt* it, and neither one of us wanted to let go. But even in the trance we were in, we still knew *where* we were, and so we (reluctantly) *relaxed, related, and released* the other.

But our eyes continued to *hold* each other as my family surrounded us and offered hugs, handshakes, and words of praise. My body had touched yet *another* new me; I had touched yet another new body *in* me. I was no longer just his student to hold up, to hold down, to hold over, to hold under, to hold in, or to hold out but someone to *hold*, someone to hold on *to*, someone to *be*hold.

And he was too.

The First Time We Kissed...

...it figures that that very afternoon, I had *to eat onions.*

I can never eat a cheeseburger without them, and if the truth be known, I shouldn't have eaten one. Mr. Reid had put me on a strict daily diet: oatmeal for breakfast; a garden salad, a vegetable plate, soup, and/or fruit for lunch; and eight glasses of water and four glasses of juice throughout the day. Most of these meals and snacks were prepared by Mr. Reid himself (the only "vegetable" one could count on the cafeteria serving was french fries), and we usually ate in his office. I could still indulge myself with chocolate cake, cookies, potato chips, and ice cream. And I was allowed to eat a cheeseburger once in a while — but *never* before a training session.

I had finished my routine, showered, and headed for his office. There were some papers he needed my mother to sign so that I could participate in the statewide gymnastics championships in Albany. I was voted the top male gymnast in Brooklyn (the first time an African-American took the title) and would be competing against four male students (all white, naturally) from the other four boroughs and thirty others from different New York counties.

I kicked my ass to earn that spot: Convinced of my talent and floored by my performance, my mother allowed me to have training sessions three hours a day, three days a week as well as on alternate Saturday mornings before afternoon choir practice (I would miss *Family Feud* and *Name That Tune* on school days and *Looney Tunes* and *Smurfs* on Saturdays, but I was more than willing to make the sacrifice). Because I was getting home at 8 o'clock on weeknights, though, she was afraid that I would slip in my grades and warned me that if I dropped in any subject, I would have to give it up. But I proved how responsible I was when I brought home all A's a week before winning the citywide competition.

That I was excelling in academics *and* athletics was still a shock to many, especially my cousin Calvin. He had to see it to believe it, and when I took my second title, he congratulated me on my floor routine with "Man, that's the best break dancin' I ever seen!" My Aunt Ruth, though, figured out one of the reasons why I had taken such an interest in athletics: "Hmm...*I* would want to be a gymnast with a coach that looked like *that*!"

I looked forward to going to Albany and bringing home title number three. That this would be my first trip outside of New York City without my mother, Aunt Ruth, or Anderson riding in the front seat was an added plus. But most important, we (meaning Mr. Reid and I) would *truly* be alone — not just in a gym, not just in another part of the city, but in another part of the *state*, for three days and two nights...*just us two.* We would finally get the chance to pick up where we left off, taking that lovely embrace we secretly shared in front of a thousand people to yet another level.

But I was really jumping the gun, because we hadn't even held hands *that way* yet, let alone kissed. You gotta crawl before you walk, right? Well, I didn't know it then, but that very day, in his office, Mr. Reid was finally going to take me out of the playpen and let me roam.

I found him standing over his desk. His office, just like the gym, had become a second home for me, so I didn't bother knocking. I closed the door and spoke to that lovely back. He was in a gray tank and shorts, courtesy of NYU.

"Hi. I'm done with my workout. Do you have the forms ready?" I looked at my watch. "If I hurry, I can catch the 6:15 bus." I placed my bag on one of his chairs and opened it.

He turned. He just looked at me. It wasn't a "something's wrong" look. It wasn't a "you caught me at a bad time" look. It wasn't a "don't you know how to knock?" look (which is what I've "seen" Anderson wear many times, since my brother and I had to get used to our mother's bedroom being his bedroom too). No, this was a look that I had seen many times on the faces of many television actors and movie stars, not to mention my mother and Anderson. A look that I never thought another man would be sporting while looking at *me*. A look...wait...he was wearing it several times today. When I managed to keep my balance while doing a straddle on the still rings. When I did a perfect dismount off the pommel horse. When I finally did that triple somersault backflip during my floor routine that we had been working on for weeks.

He held my eyes the way he did the night I won my first title. *This is it!* I screamed inside. *It's finally gonna happen!* His head bounded down on me. He sized up his target. He took aim. His lips slowly — very slowly — made their way toward mine. Our lips met — and was it ever nice to meet *his*.

I knew that you were supposed to close your eyes, but because this was my first time being kissed (those pucker-uppers as a preteen with Alvin didn't count), I didn't just want to experience it — I wanted to *see* it. I'm sure that if he had peeked at me, he probably would've laughed; my eyes were so wide, I'm sure I must have looked like an owl. I'm glad he didn't, and I'm also glad I didn't blink. I'll never forget the way his eyebrows crunched into the shape of a hump on a camel, the way his temples jumped, the way the lines formed in his forehead, the eagerness with which his soft lips touched, brushed, and claimed mine, the way his head slowly bobbed up and down, and the way his entire face seemed to glow.

After forever ended, his lips released mine, his head backed up an inch or two, and his eyes opened. There was *that* look again.

"Your lips taste like honey," he winked.

I blushed.

He took aim once again, and this time my eyes, like the rest of my body, did not stay still. My hands reached for and located his shoulders. His hands slid down to my waist. Our lips met again. And I felt the earth move again.

I wasn't about to let all that practice on Alvin and my pillow go to waste, so I let it rip. I smacked and sucked. I darted my tongue in and out of his mouth and circled his lips, which were succulently sweet.

He responded by groaning and, in one swift move, hunched down, sat back on the edge of his desk, and pulled me deeper into him by squeezing my ass. It was his turn to go to town. But he just didn't take my lips: He literally washed my mouth out with his tongue, which was also long enough to coat my throat (it tickled). I thought I was *really* gonna scream when that hot tongue made contact with my ear and he began to nip and nibble on my neck. I gladly returned the favor.

When we finished snackin' and slurpin' on each other's lips, I just stared at his chest, gently brushing that patchwork of brown hair shaped like an egg, while he looked down, tapping his feet and patting my butt with both hands (he had done this many times before, but *this* felt different this time too). This is what we both had wanted for some time, and now that it happened…we didn't have anything to say. Well, *I* sure as hell didn't know what to say. I was waiting for his cue.

With his right hand still holding on, he picked the form up off his desk with his left and handed it to me. "Make sure your mother signs both copies. Bring them back tomorrow."

That wasn't what I wanted to hear. And I didn't want to stop playing with him, but I forced myself to. He didn't speak to me in an angry tone, but it wasn't exactly cheerful either. Did I do anything wrong? Did I *not* do something he wanted me to? If I did or didn't, how would I know if he didn't *say* something?

Somewhat embarrassed and a little hurt, I took the form without looking at him. I grabbed my bag off the chair and was about to walk out without even saying good-bye — *Mitchell, you're a wreck, get it together!* — when…

"And don't you *ever* let me catch you practicing with onions on your breath again, you hear?"

Busted.

My hand on the doorknob, I turned slowly to face him.

His frown turned into a smile. He blew a kiss at me. "Put it where you want it." He winked.

I blushed.

The First Time We Slept Together...

...I also learned firsthand what they mean by the agony of defeat.

The Saturday semifinals would be a night I knew I would *never* forget. I made up my mind that I would win the title — and that Mr. Reid would win *my* title. I hadn't talked over this plan with him, but I didn't have to. As we made the trip upstate in his green Volkswagen (uh-huh, he has an affinity for compact things *and* people), I discovered a button as large as my hand inside his glove compartment: GAS, GRASS, OR ASS — NO ONE RIDES FREE.

"That means you too," he stated, not taking his eyes off the road.

"Hunh?"

"I've got a full tank. And I stopped smoking pot years ago. So you know how *you'll* have to pay." He glanced at me and grinned.

I got the message. My booty tingled.

And while we were staying in separate rooms (he had to at least make it *look* legit), he also had me to know that I would be moving into his room our last night in Albany.

'Nuff said.

I was only one of two Black male students competing, but Anton Covington, who was sporting a high-top fade a year before Olympic gold track sensation Carl Lewis made the hairstyle a fashion staple, was knocked out after the first round Friday night. That left me in the last draft, eventually challenging the all-American white boy Biff Blondell. I had to give him his props — he was good. But I knew that, given all the attention being paid to that shaggy bush of auburn brown hair, those dark blue eyes, and that nature-boy smile that, as more than one person remarked, "belonged on a tube of Crest toothpaste," I would have to outperform him *two times* just to prove that I had what it took to represent — even if I didn't *look* like it.

We had been neck and neck all night. He pulled a 9.525 on the rings; I, a 9.5 (I figured this one would go to him, since his biceps and triceps were twice the size of mine). He scored a 9.459 on the high bar; I, a 9.449. I took the parallel bars (9.565 to his 9.54) and the pommel horse (9.52 to his 9.51). And we tied on the men's floor exercise with a 9.56 (he thought he was Mikhail Baryshnikov, doing pliés to "Up Where We Belong" from *An Officer and a Gentleman,* while I twirled and tumbled to Stevie Wonder's "Ribbon in the Sky."

But then came the one event I often stumble in (literally): the vault. This shit ain't easy. You got to psyche yourself up (but not too much) before you begin to run, then psyche yourself up *to* run, then plot that run carefully up the mat, make sure you position yourself correctly so that you can jump on and off the ramp on point, onto the vault, into the air, over-under-around and over again, and land on your feet. It's that last thing that always trips me up — or, rather, makes me trip. I had never, *ever* landed on both of my feet without having to take a step backward or forward. But I was determined not to allow that to happen this time.

When it was my turn, the arena fell quiet. It was soothing — I felt as if I were all alone, like when I practice in private at school, and that took some of the pressure off of me. I rubbed chalk powder on my hands. I addressed the crowd, and I nodded at Mr. Reid. He winked and smiled; I blushed. I took two deep breaths. I sized up my target. I huffed. I gulped. I took off, and it was almost as if I were watching myself in slow motion from the sidelines...

Approaching.

Jacking.

Jumping.

Flipping.

Sailing.

Soaring.

Rolling.

Bounding.

Crunching.

Okay, okay, here I am again. I've landed.

Balance out, balance out, balance out, Lord, please let me balance out...

Will I stay grounded?

Yes!

For the first (and only) time, my landing was perfect. I came out of that mini-tuck with my feet parked in parallel, my ankles kissing, and my hands pointed and reaching so far up that I *knew* I could touch heaven.

The place went wild. Most folks, including the commentators (among them, this rather annoying announcer who relished the chance to say shit like "I don't think he'll recover from *that* move" and "This is an error that'll probably haunt him for the *rest* of his life"), concluded that I would be awarded the first and only 9.6 score of the entire weekend — as well as the title. The look on Mr. Reid's face when he sprinted toward me and tossed me in the air, screaming so loud that it scared me, told me that we had it.

But then came the score: 9.545.

I needed at least a 9.55 to overcome Biff. I knew I gave them a 9.6 and then some — and judging from the reaction of the crowd, *they* knew I did too. A loud, angry chorus of boos filled the stadium. For Christian O'Dowd, Anton's coach, it was a painful case of déjà vu: Last year, when it looked like Anton would be the top seed, he too was cut down at the wire. Was it that the judges couldn't bear sending a Negro to the national championships? As far as Christian was concerned, the answer was most definitely yes.

Yeah, we wuz robbed.

I was crushed. I was devastated. I was also somewhat humiliated: I had placed second in a contest that doesn't *have* a second place. There

was no grand-prize winner; there was no run-
ner-up (this was not the Miss America
pageant). I may as well have dropped out the
very first day of competition, since only one of
us would get to represent the state.

But I wasn't really disappointed about not
winning the title for myself. I was more upset
about disappointing Mr. Reid. All that time and
effort and energy and spirit and *love* he put into
me... While deep down I knew I wasn't at fault,
that I did my best and my best *was* the best that
I could do, I was still kicking myself inside. All
I could think was: *I brought him all this
way...to lose.*

And he must have obviously felt the same
way: He wouldn't say a word about it to me or
say a word about me or say a word about *anything*. There were just a few gestures: rubbing
my shoulder after the bad news came down,
giving me a halfhearted hug in front of the
crowd, touching the small of my back as we left
the stadium. And not once did he look me in the
eyes. *That's* what I needed, that's *all* I needed:
to look into those eyes, those reassuring eyes. I
also wanted to reassure *him:* Despite what the
judges thought, he was the best coach a student
could ever have.

But even with all the inquiries for reactions to what that asshole of a commentator referred to as "an unbelievably tragic verdict," there was nothing but the sound of solemn silence. It followed us to the hotel room. While he told Christian we might join him and Anton for a "you two should've had that shit" drink in Christian's room, even *I* knew that wasn't going to happen. He entered his room and fell facedown on the bed. Not sure of what to say or do, I just took my shower, hoping he'd come in and join me. He didn't. I put on an oversize undershirt and a pair of Fruit of the Looms. I was going to put on this cologne my mother bought for me from Avon but decided seduction was certainly the last thing on his mind, so why go through the motions?

A half hour had passed by the time I came out of the bathroom, and he was now in the middle of the bed on his back, his hands clasped behind his head, wearing just a pair of black boxer shorts. His sweat suit was folded over one of the fake-antique hotel room chairs, so I proceeded to sit in the other chair and turn on the television. I made sure the volume was low, just in case he was asleep or on his way. I sighed. Some victory celebration.

"Babe?"

Did I hear…? No. Just my imagination running away from me.

"Babe?"

There it goes again. I must *really* be in need of some comforting. I'm hearing things. I shrugged and sat back as Flo was about to tell Mel for the umpteenth time to kiss her grits.

"*Babe?* Don't you hear me calling you? Turn off the TV and come to bed."

That *was* him!

I was *gagging. He* was calling *me…that* name. I suddenly felt tingly all over. The goose bumps traveled from the tips of my toes up my back. Babe. *Babe.* He wants me to be his Babe. *His* Babe.

I gladly accepted the invitation.

I clicked off the TV. I made my way over to the bed. I climbed in, pushing my body toward him. I placed my left leg over his right leg; my right arm draped his chest, with my right hand cupping his neck. My head lay on the bed but against his side, an inch or two below his armpit. I followed his breathing.

Since he broke the silence and had ordered me to bed — an action I had no problem with — I felt I had the right to know how he felt.

"Mr. Reid?"

"Yes?"

For some reason the question I wanted to ask wouldn't come out. *This* did...

"I'm...I'm sorry."

He seemed surprised by my admission. "Sorry? Sorry about what?"

"About...about not winning."

"What do you mean?"

"I didn't win."

"Yes, you did. You're still a winner."

"I...I am?"

"Of course you are." His arms finally came down. His hands located my waist. He pulled me up and squeezed me. My head was now buried against his neck.

I sighed. "But...I feel like...like...I let you down."

"Let me down?"

"Yes. I mean—"

"Look at me, Babe."

Babe. I just loved the way it sounded, and I *loved* the way he said it. I lifted my head.

He began to stroke my face. "How could you think you let me down?"

I sighed. "Because...because you've been so quiet about it, and...I thought you were angry with me, and I..." My tears started flowing.

"Oh, Babe, don't cry." He squeezed me *tight* — tighter than he ever had before, tighter than I had ever been before. It was almost as if we had one heart.

He kissed away my tears. "How could I be angry with you? You did your very best, and that's all you could do. You didn't let me down. I'm proud of you."

"You are?"

"Yes. And *you* should be proud of yourself too. You were so good that they couldn't bear giving you the title. Your talent speaks for itself."

He kissed me. I kissed him back.

He smiled. "I know it hurts, 'cause it hurts me too. That's why I've been so quiet. I'm sorry if I made you feel I was angry with you."

It was my turn to console. I kissed his chest. "That's okay. I understand how you feel. I *know* how you feel."

"Mmm-hmm. But don't worry: We'll be back next year, and they won't have any excuse. And we ain't takin' *no* chances: You'll be doing your floor routine off of somebody *they* like."

I chuckled. "Hmm, like Joe Cocker and Jennifer Warnes?"

He laughed. "Yeah. Biff's floor routine was just fair, but that song clinched it for him.

Every time they sang 'Lift us up where we belong' and he lifted *up*, the audience screamed. But I still don't know *what* they think they're hearing when they listen to that man. He sounds constipated to me."

We laughed.

He grasped my chin, commanding my attention with those eyes. "Don't *ever* think you're letting me down. Okay?"

I nodded. "Okay."

We kissed. He shifted, opened his legs wider, and I settled between them, lying totally on top of him. I placed both my hands on his shoulders. He cupped my buns, and we snuggled close and *tight*. Our hearts beat in time.

"Good night, Babe."

I smiled. "Good night."

And I fell asleep knowing I was a winner, knowing I was a champion — especially when I was in the arms of the ultimate prize.

The First Time We Made Love...

...we didn't — but we sure did try.

After my loss at the semifinals, Mr. Reid decided that I would spend the following weekend with him. As he put it, "We still have a lot to celebrate — and there is only *one* way to celebrate."

Uh-huh...'nuff said.

But in order to make this happen, I would have to lie to my mother about my whereabouts — and I didn't feel comfortable doing this because I had never lied to her before. That's right, *never* — I never even told a "little white lie" (and while we're on this subject, can someone *please* explain to me how a lie can be *white*?). I had no reason to lie to her before (I believe that if she had had the courage to ask me if I was gay back then, I wouldn't have had the guts to say no — I would've admitted it).

So Mr. Reid stepped in and explained that we'd be going to a "physical retreat," sort of a camp for gymnasts. Such a place did exist — he produced a pamphlet about one in Hartford, Connecticut — but the only "physical retreating" we'd be doing would be to his bedroom. Because my mother had no reason to be suspicious and trusted us both, she naturally said yes. Little did she know that she was giving this man, who was twice her son's age, permission to commit a felony (for some reason, this made what we were going to do all the more exciting).

I had always been curious about the kind of life Mr. Reid lived outside of school. In the seven months that I'd known him...well, I *didn't* know him. He never talked about himself; it was always about me — my attitude, my performance, my diet. I looked forward to the day when I would finally see where he lived, how he lived, and if there was room for me.

And that day, it seemed, had *finally* come.

Mr. Reid was just as anxious as I was to get the party started: We skipped practice that Friday for the very first time (I would be getting plenty of exercise at his place anyway). He lived in Jamaica, Queens, an area that would play a significant role in my future (and not because of the obvious).

I had never been to Queens, so it was definitely an adventure for me. I immediately saw that it was a city unto itself. There were streets, roads, and avenues with the same numbers, which meant you really had to know the exact address of the residence you were visiting or you would truly be lost (92nd Avenue, 92nd Street, and 92nd Road could all be in different sections of the borough). Also, many streets are too narrow to be opened to two-way traffic — *but they are.* On more than one occasion, I just *knew* we were going to have an accident. *That* was all I needed: My mother thinks I'm out of town, turns on the 11 o'clock news, and discovers that I was en route to my coach's house for a rendezvous.

We stopped off at a grocery store (where, among other things, he purchased two packages of Fig Newtons, his favorite snack) and a fruit and vegetable stand. The vendor — an Asian man Mr. Reid addressed as Rocky — sized me up: "Oh…is this, uh, the young man?"

"Yes," Mr. Reid smiled. *"This* is him."

Hmm…he's been talking to folks — or at least one person — about me. But what did he say? And what did he refer to me as: his student, his (soon-to-be) lover, or both? Knowing that I was a topic of conversation outside the school made me tingle.

Mr. Reid lived in a one-bedroom apartment located on the top floor of a ten-story co-op. I was impressed: There was a doorman, a recreation area, a laundry service, and 24-hour parking *underneath* the dwelling. While these features were a clear sign that he led a glamorous life (and naturally made me wonder how he could afford such a place on a teacher's salary), that notion was dispelled the moment I stepped inside his apartment.

Save a framed poster of Muhammad Ali in *The Greatest* and a black-velvet painting of what appeared to be two nude, beautifully sculpted Black men in a rather suggestive embrace hanging over his leather love seat, his emerald-green walls were bare. There weren't pictures of him or anyone else anywhere. There was one small two-level bookcase that sat on the left side of the love seat (only five books were stacked on its top: *Roots, Invisible Man, Manchild in the Promised Land, Brave New World*, and *1984*). There were

no lamps — just two sets of track lights on opposite sides of the living room. A wooden rocking
chair sat in one corner, while a very big, very
scary-looking cactus plant sat in another. A stereo
system with an audiocassette deck and an eight-
track player sat opposite the love seat.

"Why don't you make yourself comfortable,
put on some music while I tend to this?" he
suggested, heading for the kitchen.

I did as I was told. I kicked off my shoes, allow-
ing my feet to melt into the light brown carpet. I
checked out his record collection. It certainly was
a mixed bag: Alongside the O'Jays, Eddie
Kendricks, Joan Armatrading, Al Jarreau, the
Commodores, Roy Ayers, Charley Pride, Isaac
Hayes, Sly and the Family Stone, the Pointer
Sisters, Parliament/Funkadelic, and Jimi Hendrix
were Linda Ronstadt, James Taylor, Phoebe Snow,
the Doobie Brothers, Fleetwood Mac, Emmylou
Harris, Chicago, Rickie Lee Jones, Steely Dan, the
Police, Three Dog Night, and Kenny Rogers. And
these were just in the first pile I glanced at — there
were four other milk crates filled with LPs, two
sitting on each side of the stereo.

I came across a name that sounded familiar,
but the face didn't go with the name. And then
it clicked.

"Why didn't you tell me Randy Crawford was a singer...and that *he* is a *she*?" I called out to him.

"Because I knew you would visit one day and find out," he answered.

I blushed.

Randy's album had an interesting lineup of songs: Keith Carradine's "I'm Easy," Paul Simon's "Something So Right," Elton John's "Don't Let Me Down." I figured out how to work the stereo and turned her on. I then joined him in the kitchen. His hardwood floors were sparkling-clean and cold. My mother would kill for the accessories he had: a refrigerator that makes ice cubes, a dishwasher, and a garbage disposal. He already had most of the groceries put up.

He heard the beginning strands and smiled. "Ah, that was a good selection." The selection in question was "Everything Must Change." Uh-huh, everything must change...*that* would be another hard lesson I would learn with him.

"Can I help with anything?" I offered.

"Can you cook?"

"Of course I can. You forget that I was once a latchkey kid."

"Okay. Let's see..." He placed his hands on his hips. He frowned. "I know." He moved me in front of the sink (no, I didn't mind being manhandled). "You can cut the potatoes and onions while I season the chicken."

"Now, why do *I* get the hard job and *you* get the easy one?" I sulked.

"You *have* the easy job," he argued. He held me from behind. "There is a special art to seasoning meat. And I have to make my special sauce to baste it. But don't worry: *You'll* find out about *that* later on."

Yeah, I would.

I rolled up my sleeves, washed my hands, and went to work. I was spending more time watching him, though. I got to know Randy's voice — sexy, supple, and sweet — and enjoyed listening to him whistle along. By the time side one ended, everything was in the oven and the broccoli was ready to be steamed.

"Why don't you wait in the living room while I just tidy up a bit," he said.

Once again I did as I was told. I didn't know exactly what to do with myself, though. Should I just sit on the love seat and strike a seductive pose? Or should I play the coquette, parking it in the rocking chair and waiting to be summoned? I decided to do neither. I put on side two of Randy and stood over the stereo as I studied the other two Randy Crawford albums I discovered.

The sun was beginning to set, so he turned on his track lights. He then kicked off his sneakers and socks, pulled off his T-shirt, and stretched out on the carpet on his back.

He sighed. "Why don't you join me down here?"

I turned. I smiled. I did.

I lay on top of him and finally got to ask my twenty questions. He was born and raised in Kansas City, Missouri, "the city that has more water fountains than Paris and more boulevards than Rome." He's the oldest of four, the only son. His mother was a dancer but gave it up to be a housewife while his father pursued a successful military career (a graduate of West Point who did a stint at Fort Bliss, he's a three-star general). He left home at seventeen without the blessing of his father (who wasn't pleased his son didn't want to follow in his footsteps), hitchhiking his way to UCLA, where he attended classes on an athletic scholarship (he didn't say, but I gathered by the mood he relayed this story in that, because of his choice, father and son are still estranged). He got his degree in physical therapy (that accounts for those healing hands) and became a reflexologist (i.e., personal trainer and masseur) for the Los Angeles

Lakers for four years (uh-huh, he clocked dumb dollars). He's lived in New York for five years and has taught phys ed at Morrow for four. He never mentioned a boyfriend or girl-friend — past or present — and I was too chicken to ask.

We ate by candlelight at his three-piece glass dining set, which IKEA would be famous for a decade later. He filled me in on some of the goings-on at the school, such as Ms. Funicello's tendency to nip the gin before every class and the affair Mr. Marcelli, the astronomy teacher, and Ms. Benson, a guidance counselor, were having (of course, I wondered if *our* affair might be discussed at someone's dinner table too).

After the dishes were put in the dishwasher, we had dessert: a bowl of strawberries and grapes. But *we* didn't eat — he did. I sat on the carpet in a lotus position and fed him while he lay on his stomach, his head resting on me. It was then his turn to quiz me with twenty questions.

When all the fruit was gone, he took the bowl and headed into the kitchen. I thought he was going to get some more. But he turned off the kitchen light, returned without the bowl, and headed straight for the stereo. He found an album and put it on.

He bent down on one knee and smiled. "Would you like to dance with me?"

I gasped. "Uh…yeah."

He held out his hand. I took it. He lifted me up off the carpet. He stooped so I could wrap my arms around his neck. He pulled me into him.

I had never slow-danced with anyone before, male or female, so I just followed his lead. But his feet weren't doing the groovin' — his hips were. This, of course, made me stiff. I tried to get my mind off my hard-on — *and* his.

"Uh, is this Randy?" I asked.

"No. It's Anita Baker."

"Anita Baker? Hmm, I've never heard of her."

"Well, she's a new artist. This is her first album."

"Oh. What's the name of the album?"

"*The Songstress.*"

You could say that again: The lady could *sang*. As Anita serenaded us with "Angel," he whistled it. I wanted so badly to ask if that was what I was to him, but I didn't. The next song, "You're the Best Thing Yet," could've been a "Quiet Storm" dedication from me to him. And we did exactly what the final two songs declared: "Feel the Need" and "Squeeze Me."

But when the music stopped, we didn't. We kept on feelin' and squeezin', slow-jammin' to the sounds our bodies were makin'.

And then…

"Babe?" he whispered.

"Yes?" I breathed.

His tongue made contact with my ear. "Let's take a shower together."

I felt like screaming *I thought you'd never ask!* but mouthed "Okay" instead. We broke apart. I squeezed his hand tight as he led me to the bathroom, turning off the track lights on the way.

The walls, the towels and washcloths, the carpet, his robe, even his toothbrush and the toilet tissue were ocean-blue. The scent that filled the air seemed to be one of ammonia…and strawberries.

He undressed me, allowing his fingers and hands to cup, caress, and creep. When he parted my cheeks to stroke my insides, I just knew I was gonna cum right then.

When he stepped back and stepped out of his jeans and boxers, I *gasped*. This was the very first time I was seeing him totally naked, and I just knew I was going to lose it. He was such a magnificent sight. And his dick — a shade darker than the rest of him — was pointed straight at me. I looked at it — and him — with longing and lust.

He laughed. He grabbed it, making me jump. "You don't have to be afraid to touch it. You don't have to be afraid to touch *me*. After all, you're going to wash me."

With that he pulled back the glass door, adjusted the water, and ushered me into the tub. He backed me under the water, ducking down so that he too could join me. He held me and kissed me for the second time.

Yeah, it was better than the first.

He gave me my own bar of soap to rub-a-dub-dub him up. I didn't miss one part of his body (I even cut his pound cakes and made sure they were totally covered with icing). But I most enjoyed what he did to me. He managed to get two fingers inside me; I shivered and quivered.

But the ultimate high came — *literally* — when he washed my dick and ended up jerking me off. Ooh, Lord, could he *beat it*! With his hand pumpin', the soap foamin', the water sprinklin', his dick pressin' up against my ass, his hot breath blowin', and his voice groanin' "Yeah, Babe, come on, now, come *on*" — the shit was so good that I *hated* it. Uh-huh, you know it's Good with a c-a-p-i-t-a-l *G* when you *fightin'* it. I kept pushing him away, even yelling "No!" It never felt like this when I did it, and I really believed that nothing could — that nothing *should* — feel *this* Good.

But I was no match for him, and I'm glad I wasn't: He held on to me and held on to *it*. I finally let out a cry that seemed to come from somewhere else but inside me, hit an octave or two, and gargled as if I were drowning as he tugged on my dick like I was a cow with an udder, watching my milk spurt up and onto the glass door.

After a workout like that, I was ready to faint, so it was a good thing he was still holding me up. I had never cum before like that (and never thought I *could*). I was kind of embarrassed. He continued to stroke it while kissing my neck.

"So...I guess I don't have to ask if you enjoyed that, hunh?" he asked.

I looked up at him. We both looked at the glass. We laughed.

We rinsed each other off as well as the glass. We stepped out of the shower. I was about to reach for a towel hanging on the rack when he stopped me. "No. We won't need one."

And we didn't. He cut off the bathroom light and scooped me up in his arms. Since his hands were full carrying me, he had me hit a switch as we entered his bedroom. A green tint bounced off the light brown–colored walls, making the room hazy and cozy. A queen-size bed was positioned in the middle of the room, with an eight-drawer wooden dresser sitting in a corner opposite the foot of the bed. This is where he put me down.

Have you ever been blown dry? Your body is wet, and that human wind is warm. He turned me, he folded me, he *spread* me…and *blew*.

Lawdy.

And then his lips *really* got down to bizness.

Lick me. Suck me. Puck me. *Eat* me.

Up…down.

Over…under.

Inside…out.

Lawdy, lawdy.

Mmm-hmm. Circle my belly button.

Oh, yeah. Nip that nipple.

Oh, my God. Is he…is he…? He *is*. Now, I had heard people say *kiss my ass* many times, but I never thought anybody actually did that. *Ooh. Ah, yeah.* How many licks does it take to get to the Tootsie Roll center of *my* Tootsie Pop? I don't know, but keep on bastin' and tastin' it with that special sauce, and I'm *sure* you'll find out!

Oh, shit! Slurp on my big toe and fuck me with your thumb, why don'tcha!

I didn't want it to end — I mean, my booty was burnin'! — but I was feelin' so damn Good that I didn't want to be selfish. I wanted to give him some of what I was gettin'. And while he was dry by the time his turn came, he was wet again by the time I was done. The flavor was butterscotch, and was he tay-stee!

My exploration was thorough — at least in the front. I never got a chance to taste the backhand side because I made the mistake of swallowing him whole — an action that took us *both* by surprise.

"Oh, Babe!" he screamed, gripping my head, pushing it down, and thrusting his body forward.

No, I didn't really mean to do it. As I was making my way down from his belly button, doin' my own tongue dance, there it was, just *staring* at me. How could I pass it up? I was just planning on taking a lick or two...or three. Stealing a kiss or puckering it up. But...what can I say? I was greedy.

I was shocked that I was able to take it all in one swoop. I mean, he wasn't exactly small (looking back, I'd say he was nine inches on the Dickter scale, with a round-the-way feel of about five). Also, I had never done that before.

But as my actions made clear, I was one eager beaver.

I paced myself: easing down, easing up. Easing down. Easing up. *Easy...down. Easy...up.*

"*Uh-huh, uh-huh, uhhh-huhhh,*" he called.

Sop every drop. Lip every drip. And keep on shuckin' it to the cob.

"*Hum-a-nah-hum-a-nah-hum-a-nah-hum-a-nah,*" he mumbled like Ralph Kramden on *The Honeymooners.*

Heave. Heave. *Heave...ho!*

"*Please, Babe, stop!*" he moaned, trying to push me off of him.

I wouldn't budge. I mean, even *I* knew that when they are yelling *no,* they really mean *yes.*

But then...

"*No!*" his entire body screamed, tossing me off of him and onto the floor. I landed on my back.

I got up and found him jerking as if he were having a fit. Well, in a way, he was. He had his arms out for me.

He was out of breath. "Babe? Babe, you okay?"

I sat on top of him, grinning. "I should be asking *you* that."

"I...I'm sorry. It's just that...you were taking me to the bridge, and...and we haven't got to the second verse yet. I wanted to save *that* kind of finish for when we make love."

"Oh. I'm sorry." I stroked both of his heads.

"Ooh...whew...don't be sorry. You sure knew what to do down there. Sure you haven't had any practice?"

"What do you think I was doing?"

"Ah, you get lucky your first time, and now you want to be cocky about it, hunh?"

I put my hands on my hips. "Luck? *That* was skill."

He eased up; he had this look that said I was in trouble. "Oh, you think so, hunh?"

I got the message; I began inching my way up to the head of the bed. "Uh...uh...yeah."

He pounced, trapping me. His action was so aggressive and his expression so frightening — it reminded me of Jack Nicholson coming after Shelley Duvall in *The Shining* — that I let out a scream that made *my* blood curdle.

He was enjoying this. "Uh-huh. Don't let your mouth get you into something your *ass* can't get you out of." He slid his hands down there.

I was speechless. "I, uh, um, I..."

He let out a laugh that was identical to Vincent Price's à la Michael Jackson's "Thriller." He held my gaze. "I think it's time to take the lid off the cookie jar…don't you?"

He waited for me to answer. I didn't. He began to nod. I hesitantly nodded along with him. He smiled. I did too.

Then, without warning, he threw my legs up and started tastin' and bastin' that booty again. By the time he was done, I was on my stomach, and my ass — so hot even *I* could smell the smoke — was rumped up and rarin' to go.

And he knew it. "Just hold on, Babe," he said, climbing off of me, leaving me looking (and *feeling*) very naked. "I have to get a Trojan."

Now, we were doing this BC — that's *before condoms* — but I guess Mr. Reid thought enough of me (or was it himself?) to use one (I'd later learn that he loved the extra friction a condom created, pulling on his very tight foreskin while his dick staked its claim inside me). I don't remember ever hearing the words "GRID" or "AIDS" back then — and, believe it or not, I didn't know what a condom was (and why would I, since my sex-ed teacher, Mr. Bannister, couldn't say "sexual intercourse," not to mention "penis" and "vagina," without blushing).

So, yes, I looked at him, puzzled. "A Trojan?"

"Yes. A rubber."

"A rubber? What's that?"

"*What's that?* You…you don't know what a *rubber* is?"

Uh-huh, I *really* felt stupid. All I could do was shrug.

He chuckled. "*Damn.* I'm not only breaking the seal, I must be breaking the *mold* too, hunh?"

I shrugged again.

I watched as he took the rubber out of its wrapper and carefully placed and rolled it on. *It* was larger and thicker than I had ever seen it, and I was surprised something as small and thin as a condom could fit Mr. Big Stuff. I mean, it's rubber, it can stretch, but I just knew it was going to pop or break, but it didn't. And, at that moment, it dawned on me that he was going to put *all that* in me.

Yeah…I started to have second thoughts.

He must have sensed this. He climbed on top of me, taking aim, and looped his arms under mine. "You okay?"

"Uh…yeah."

"You sure? We don't have to right now. We have the whole weekend."

That was my cue to bow out, but for some reason I felt I owed it to him to try. "No, no. I want to. It's just that...well..."

"You're worried it'll hurt, right?"

"Uh...yeah."

"Don't worry. If it hurts, we'll stop, okay?"

I nodded. He tried getting my mind off of *it* by tonguing me down and playing with my nipples. It worked...somewhat. I knew that with every kiss, with every nip, *it* was inchin', pushin' its way deeper into me. Every thrust was good to him; I could tell by the "Oh, Babe" he would sigh. But it *hurt*. I couldn't *relax, relate, or release,* so I tightened up — and that didn't make its entry any easier.

He figured out that he was enjoying this more than I was. He pulled out (or, rather, up, since he wasn't even *in* to begin with), rimming me before he lay back down on me.

"Babe, you tighter than the skin on a conga drum. But it's okay, it's all right," he whispered, lightly kissing my face. He then aimed for my lips; I gave them to him.

I stared at the pillow I was lying on. "I'm...I'm sorry."

He chuckled. "Sorry? Sorry about what?"

I glanced at him through the corner of my eyes. "That I...I can't do it."

"You don't have anything to be sorry about, Babe," he consoled. "You can do it, and we will." His dick agreed: It began to throb between my butt cheeks.

"But I don't know," I said, still unsure. "I mean, I...I...the pain...it hurts...and...I want to, but—"

"Sh," he whispered, placing his right thumb on my lips. "We got time, Babe. And we don't have to do it in that position if you don't want. There are other ways."

"There are?" I asked, very naive.

"Yeah," he responded with disbelief in his voice. "You really *are* a virgin, hunh?"

We grinned.

"I know what you *can* do for me — and you don't have to move."

"What?"

He eased up. "Close your legs." I complied. He locked his thighs around mine and his arms up and under my arms.

"Are you comfortable?" he asked.

Am I comfortable? Is he kidding? How could I *not* be with this big hunk of man on top of me and *that* poking me, just itchin' to get inside?

I just smiled. "Yes, I am."

"I'm not crushing you, am I?"

"No." And even if he were, I wouldn't care. He's the best kind of blanket.

"Okay." He kissed me. "Good night, Babe."

"Good night."

And it *was* a good night. Sleep came so easy. I didn't mind that he snored just a little too loud. If it were my brother, I would've tapped him to turn over. But the sounds he made were more like music. He was out before me, so I just listened to him. It was like a lullaby. Yeah, it put me to sleep.

I woke up the next morning to that musical sound. I just watched him sleep and thought about what could've been last night. I hated myself for getting cold feet. I know he wouldn't have been pleased to know I was going down that road again, but I still felt I let him down...*again*. This time, of course, it wasn't about showin' the judges and the crowds what I could do on the mat; it was about showin' this man that I knew I loved, that I knew I was in love with, how much I loved and was in love with him. And I wasn't about to let a little pain get in the way again.

So, holding on to his arms and crossing my legs around his, I woke him up with a little bump 'n' grind.

"Mmm," he groaned. "Good morning."

"Good morning."

We kissed.

He returned the bump. "Well, it certainly feels like *you* are up and at 'em and ready to go."

"It feels like you are too." And it certainly did.

"So you want to eat breakfast before we try again?"

"I don't need breakfast. I have enough energy," I declared.

His eyebrows raised. "Oh, do you?"

"Yes," I cooed.

"You sure that's *you* talking and not just *that?*" He bumped my booty.

I returned his bump and tongued him. "Yes."

He got the message. He rolled off of me again. He opened and reached inside the dresser drawer again. He pulled out another rubber. He searched another drawer and produced what looked like a tube of toothpaste (it was K-Y jelly). I sat up and watched him put on the rubber. He then sat down at the head of the bed and motioned for me to come to him.

"Let's try it this way," he suggested. I took his hands.

"This way" amounted to sitting on it. He inched his way down a little. He had me squat in front of him. He squirted some lubricant on the tips of his fingers on his right hand and began greasing me up. *Ooh*…it was cool, and it gave me goose bumps. He then carefully maneuvered his middle finger inside me, and I lost my balance a few times — but not because it hurt. *This* is what we were missing last night; the shit felt *too* Good.

When he figured I was ready (and I was), he stopped. He clutched my waist. I continued to hold on to his shoulders while he put my ass in sync with his dick.

"Now, you guide it in, Babe."

I was dumbstruck. *Me? Guide it in?* He brings me all this way, and now he was gonna leave me out here to decide what to do next? I just nodded and started to feel my way around him. I began to come in for what I knew would be my first of many landings when my right foot slipped and I had all of him — *all of him* — inside me.

I freaked out. *"Oh, no, oh, no!"*

He stopped me from getting up and kissed my face all over. "Oh, Babe, just relax. It's in, it's in, don't pull up. You got through the hard part. *Ah*, it feels *so* good. *You* feel so good. Just relax. Relate. Release."

103

Uh-huh, easy for him to say — *he* wasn't being invaded. I had no one but myself to blame, though: I had let my mouth get me into something my ass might not be able to get me out of. *I'm* the one who asked for it, and he gave it to me — *So, Mitchell, what are you gonna do with it?*

Maybe he was right: The hard part may be over (and it was *hard*). I wasn't about to strike out a second time. I had come this far — by faith? — and couldn't turn back now.

So I let go and let God.

I closed my eyes and began to breathe the way I would before I attempted a movement or stunt that was difficult. I then realized that — surprise, surprise — *it didn't hurt!* I mean, it didn't exactly feel Good (or good), but there was no pain. Just a little discomfort.

I raised my behind up and down, getting used to this new sensation. I didn't know if I liked what I was feeling (and I couldn't even describe it if you asked me), but *he* sure did.

"*Ooh, yeah, Babe,*" he groaned, his eyes closed. "Ah, you so nice and tight."

I was, so I decided to experiment. I slowly began working my hips front to back. It was the right move.

"Damn, Babe. Mmm-hmm." He followed my lead, humping as I swung low. I could *really* feel something now, and, yeah, I *loved* it. Every time we met on the downstroke, I would sigh an *"uh"* and he an *"ooh."*

I was comfortable enough to let go of his shoulders and place my palms on the bed. I changed to a counterclockwise movement (why, I don't know) as he sat back on his elbows.

"Yeah, Babe. Rock me gently. Rock me slowly."

I did. But after a while I had to pick up that pace: I had never felt anything like this before and (at the time) never thought I would again. I had to take *all* I could and went for mine. I imagined I was on the pommel horse and pommeled him into the bed, jocking and jostling with delight. At one point my legs were around his neck as I, as he put it, "row, row, rowed your boat."

I kept rowin', and he kept *growin'*. My grunts became gruesome; so did his. My heaves were husky and heavy; so were his. I teetered, he tottered. He seemed somewhat shocked and surprised: That look said, *I didn't think you'd get the hang of it that quick!* But I did. I was serious about gettin' that nut. We were *not* gonna have a repeat performance from last night: I was in it to win it.

As serious as I was, though, there was room for some humor. While he laughed at my tongue (which uncontrollably wagged as if I were a dog panting for water), I laughed as his head kept hitting the bed's headboard. I must have laughed a little too much and one time too many at him over that, though: He proceeded to up the ante by grabbing my dick, greasing it up with lubricant, and jerking me off. That really set *me* off: I started to pound wildly, jumping, jacking, jump-jacking until…

I started making noises like Hoperoo on *The Flintstones* and erupted like Mount St. Helens.

Now, this explosion topped last night's: I had never cum so much *and* so long before. It was thick and gooey, completely covering my dick and his hand (which was still pumping me).

I was still springing that major leak when he pulled out of me and pulled off the condom. *"Ay, ay, ay, ay, ay!"* he exclaimed like Ricky Ricardo, tuggin' and chuggin' on his dick.

And then…

"Grrra-a-a-u-u-u-ggghhh."

Uh-huh, he blew his top too. I watched as it spurted out, in fountainlike fashion (uh-huh, just like a man from Kansas City), in all directions — on his chest, on his legs, on the bed, and on me. Squeezin' my own thang, I got up and sucked his right nipple. He howled and I growled as we and our dicks came down.

Looking at the mess we made, we grinned.

"I guess we were both savin' it up, hunh?" he asked.

I nodded a smile. I kissed him and pulled him down on top of me. I wrapped my legs around his waist. We stirred in our natural juices, marinating in the other's special sauce, all sticky and sweaty, until...

"Babe?"

"Yes?"

"Can I ask you a question?"

"Yes."

"Uh...are you *sure* you were a virgin?"

"What do you mean?"

"What I mean is...well...last night you showed all the signs. *But just now?* You...you were *workin'* it — and workin' *me* over."

"I was?"

"*Hell, yeah!* You just took this bull by his horn," he said, thrusting it against me, "and rode 'im like you were a rodeo champion."

I giggled. "Well, I *am* a champion, remember?"

"Ha, I know."

We kissed.

"Thank you, Babe."

"For what?"

"For that good, *good* lovin'."

"Well, you gotta give it to get it. I did have some help."

He smiled.

"Are you sure I did good?" I asked.

"Hell, yeah." He sighed. "But I'll know better next time."

"Know what?"

"If I'm gonna make love with you in the morning, I *better* have breakfast first!"

We giggled.

Himnastics

So how Good *was* the sex?

Hindsight *is* twenty-twenty, and while today I can say that it wasn't *the* best ever (yes, my Pooquie holds that title now), it is still way above the rest of my other sexperiences.

In a nutshell:

It was better than getting my allowance every Friday.

It was better than scoring a 1450 on my SATs.

It was better than reading a James Baldwin novel (and that's *really* sayin' somethin') and *much* better than reading about it in a copy of *Jive, Bronze Thrills,* or *Black Confessions* (ain't nuthin' like the real thing, baby).

It was better than a tall, cool, iced-to-the-bone glass of Aunt Ruth's homemade lemonade on a maxed-out-mercury, triple-digit, blazin'-saddles hot day.

It was better than a double-Dutch-fudge chocolate-chip ice-cream sundae with rainbow sprinkles and whipped cream.

It was better than waking up in the morning to the smell of bacon and eggs (nobody cooks 'em like Mom does).

It was better than hearing my mother and Anderson do it. Thinking my brother and I were asleep, he would be so loud that my mother would spend half the time shushing him, warning him, "You'll wake the kids." Ha, little did she know we were enjoyin' the show...

It was better than *beatin' it* while gazing at my posters of Foster Sylvers (yes, from the group that gave us that all-time classic "Boogie Fever"), Ron Glass from *Barney Miller* (Lord, could that man wear a double-breasted suit!), and Erik Estrada, Ponch of *CHiPs* (he could patrol my highways and byways anytime!).

It was better than finally seeing Krystle Carrington knock the shit out of Alexis Colby on *Dynasty*.

It was better than watching Dorothy Dandridge turn lip synchin', eye battin', and hip holdin' into art forms in *Carmen Jones*.

It was better than listening to Aretha — and up until then I never thought anybody or anything could give me the chills, give me a thrill, just go in for the *kill* the way she does, wailin' on "Ain't No Way" (with Cissy Houston hitting *the* notes of all time) or testifyin' on "Dr. Feelgood" (that's the *Live at Fillmore West* version, not the original).

And I know this is really gonna sound sacrilegious, but it was better than catchin' the Holy Ghost on Sunday morning (mmm-hmm...I now had a new reason to feel the spirit, ya know what I'm sayin'?).

After showing me all the right moves on the mat, Mr. Reid *really* put those principles of balance, flexibility, strength, and spatial awareness to work. The muscles and the movements, the angles and the arches, the stances and the stations, the positions and the places...they all came together as we came together, without apology, without shame, without guilt (hell, if what we had, if what we shared, if what we *were* together was wrong in the eyes of any man, any woman, any God, so be it; anything this Good couldn't be bad).

That first time — I'm going to once again go

out on a religious limb here — was like a bap-
tism. He washed me — not whiter than snow (I
have always refused to sing that hymn in church
for reasons I'm sure I don't have to explain) but
with a melanin sun. So orange, so brown, so
bright, so strong. Like a river of wet dreams, of
wet streams, splashing away the remnants of the
innocence I once had, replacing it with a fever, a
fervor, a flavor for sensuality and seduction, for
the wondrous and the wicked, for all the lust I
could crave and all the love I could carry. It was
my initiation into adulthood, into manhood,
into the African communion.

He took me there.

No, I don't exactly know where *there* was,
but if your first time was as Good as mine, I
think you know where I'm coming from. It isn't
special just because it's your first time; it's special because of who it was with and where you
went together (and did we take a trip!).

Thanks to Mr. Reid, my "nothing book" really became a *something book*. Instead of sharing
fantasies with my journal every night, lusting
after the bus driver on my school route or the
stock boy at the supermarket or the barber who
does my brother's hair or the model in the liquor
ad in *Jet* or the mechanic fixing my mother's car

or the superintendent unclogging our drain or the telephone man checking our line or the salesman at the shoe store (I could certainly go on and on and *on;* I fell in lust with someone new every day), I could *finally* say that the fantasy was now a reality. I no longer had to wonder what having a guy in my life would be like, what being *with* a guy would be like.

And, *My Guy,* he definitely knows how to…

Fortify

Signify

Satisfy

Sanctify

Electrify

Simplify

Justify

Pacify

Qualify

Quantify

Terrify

Mystify

Mesmerize

Energize

Tantalize

Tranquilize

Edify

Codify

Purify

Beautify

...me.

And now that I've found him, now that I *have* him...

I Feel Pretty

Uh-huh...pretty, witty, *and* gay.

I had my very first boyfriend — a high school sweetheart. No, he didn't put a ring on my finger, I wasn't wearing his school varsity jacket (not that he had one for me to wear), and he didn't officially ask me to go steady, but his actions — *our* actions — told the story.

When he held my eyes, he was *really* holding my eyes.

When he held my hand, he was *really* holding my hand.

And when he held me in his arms, he was *really* holding me in his arms.

Naturally, we had to be extra careful that no one could detect what was going on. We had to catch ourselves many times — either I was staring a little too hard or he was squeezing the Charmin just a little too long.

And sometimes I had to wear T-shirts and sweatpants instead of tank tops, shorts, or a bodysuit to class to hide the love bites he gave me all over my body (I didn't have to worry about the hickeys on my butt).

Most of our rendezvous would happen at school, on a Tuesday, Friday, or Saturday before or after practice on the fifth-floor gym, which was never used. No one was allowed up there, probably because it was so isolated from the rest of the school. Only the custodians had access to it (as well as the stairwell that led to it), but they had no reason to go up there.

Guess who else had a key?

I didn't know how he got one, and quite frankly, I didn't care. He made me a copy, and if that day was the day (and it usually was), he'd say, "Meet me at..." And like clockwork I'd be on time, and he'd be waiting for me. He kept it fresh, funky, and *sexsational*. He put my body to work — pulling, pressing, binding, stretching me like a rubber band, like a human Slinky. It was fitting that the only piece of equipment in that gym was a pommel horse. Ya know we just went buck wild on it (uh-huh, let me ride that pony express!).

And it's a good thing that gym was so far from the rest of civilization, because we made some *noise*.

Now, what we had was very much physical (and since I was such a horny teen, that wasn't a problem for me). But we did share a lot with our clothes *on*.

Like when he taught me how to use chopsticks. We were on what I considered our first date, to celebrate our birthdays (mine being April fifteenth; his, April twenty-eighth): a movie (*Flashdance*) and dinner (a Chinese restaurant called Charlie Mom in the Village). I made sure my ensemble was clean, pressed, and *sharp* — a lime-green Izod shirt, my very first pair of Gap khakis (I decided my Lee jeans were not formal enough for the occasion), and Thom McAn brown loafers, which I shined to a sparkle — and I splashed my entire body with some of Anderson's aftershave. He liked the outfit (especially the way the pants hugged my booty) and said the cologne was sexy (after it settled, it began to itch, so I couldn't wait to get to his place and let him wash it all off).

But he got real excited — *bewildered* — when, on my first try, I was eating with the sticks like a pro ("You just don't like being a virgin at *anything*, do you?").

He loved to watch classic thrillers on TV, such as *Them!* and *Invasion of the Body Snatchers* or anything starring Vincent Price, with *House on Haunted Hill, House of Wax*, and, of course, *The Fly* high on his list of faves. I lied about not seeing most of them and often faked being scared so that he would hold me closer. I would let out one of those hair-raising screams like those silly-ass white women in the flicks (if it was a sister, she just wouldn't stand, lie, or sit and watch the damn monster attack her and wait for "the man" to save her; she'd be kicking up some dirt and fighting for dear life!).

And he loved to play backgammon. He taught me how to play, and before long I was trouncing him. But that didn't matter, for any-time I beat him he'd exact his revenge on me by putting a serious beatin' on me with his thang.

No, I didn't complain.

In addition to being my lover, my playmate, my friend, and a father figure (because he is seven years younger than my mother, Anderson seemed more like a sibling than an elder), Mr. Reid was also my hero. He was there for me during two of the most traumatic experiences of my life.

He came to hear me sing in church. It was my very first time as a soloist, and I was a nervous wreck. I had sung solo before but always had folks backing me up. Not this time. I knew the song, "Rescue Me," by Tramaine Hawkins, by heart. But I also knew that my performance would be enhanced if I had all the moral support I could get — in other words, if "my man" was somewhere in the congregation.

It was in the summer, a week after my mother ceased being a widow and became Mrs. Annie Walker. Like Mr. Reid, Anderson wasn't much of a churchgoer but made the trip to please my mother. But he always made his disdain for our pastor, the Reverend Alexander Pierce Gooding, known. "He's full of somethin', and it *ain't* the Holy Ghost," he often said before and after Sunday service. I had to agree but for different reasons.

For Anderson, Reverend Gooding was no good because he spent too much of the church's money on everything but the church (as he's asking members to "dig down *deep* in your pockets for that little extra somethin' for the Lawd," his wife and six kids are all sporting new coats, new hats, and new outfits, courtesy of last week's diggin'-down-deeper session).

For me, Reverend Gooding was no good because he was so bad. When he said "Let me pray on you," he wanted to *prey* on you. When he said "Let me lay hands on you," he wanted to lay his hands *all* over you. I had been touched, felt, squeezed, and pinched many times by him, and now that my body was more tight and taut, it was happening even more frequently (like every Sunday). He would, no doubt, be "making his move" soon — like he had with about half of the other Young Adult Choir's male members. I had been warned a few years ago. But while most of the other members would surrender to his advances (they were aching for affection and seduced by his standing), I wouldn't — especially since I had someone to fulfill those needs.

He was in rare form this particular morning — calling on "Gawd" to design and deliver, dabbing the sweat off his forehead with the handkerchiefs he had in each hand. He pumped up the congregation for my debut.

"Brothers and sisters, we are *really* going to have *shuhsh* this mo'nin'. Ya heard me? Not church. I'm talkin' *shuhsh*. One of our young disciples is going to come forth and offer us praise in song. And Lawd knows that it *is* the children that will lead us.

So let us worship Him. Brother Crawford? Come and tell us what He's done for *you*."

He held out his arms. I rose out of my seat as the "amens" filled the house. I reluctantly put my arms around his neck as he pulled me into him. "Now, let us *feel* it," he whispered in my ear. Ha, *he* was already feeling it, and he was letting *me* feel it too: His dick was singing its *own* song.

He released me (finally), and I stepped up to the microphone. Our musician, Mr. Browning, began to play, and I scanned the congregation for Mr. Reid. Just before I began the first verse, he appeared at the back of the church, looking too *p-h-y-n-e* in a white shirt, paisley blue tie, and navy blue slacks. He caught my eyes and gave me that baby-grand grin I thought belonged only to my second-grade teacher, Mr. Weatherspoon.

Yeah, I got inspired.

My eyes settled and stayed on him throughout the whole song. I did a few runs, worked a melisma, and even hit an octave — something that caused my mother, whose joy in church was often contained, to shout, "Thank you, Jesus!" By the end of the song, I was in tears, and so was the entire Young Adult Choir and many of the members. But while they thought I was singin' about Jesus, I was really singin' about, for, and to my man (yeah, I know — just blasphemous).

I did believe that, in his own way, Mr. Reid *had* "rescued me." But a couple of months later, he got to do just that — literally.

It was a Friday afternoon. I was warming up (or, rather, showing off) on the balance beam, doing handstands, not really watching what I was doing, when I went to do a cartwheel and my hands didn't land on the beam. I went tumbling and, in an effort to try and break my fall, crunched my body and covered my head as I landed on the mat. My left leg hit one of the metal poles attached to the beam.

I screamed so loud that Mr. Reid said he heard me on the first floor (the gym was on the third floor). When I went to reach for my left ankle, I saw nothing but blood — and fainted.

The next thing I remember was "feeling" picked up, carried, and taken. The nurse's office at school was closed, so he ran me straight to the public hospital, which was a few blocks away. He didn't know how much damage was done and didn't want to waste any time trying to transport me there by car.

He lied and told the doctor that I was his nephew; they believed him. My injury wasn't serious even though it scared us both. No bones were broken, no ligaments or muscles were torn, but the gash going from the ball of my foot past my ankle would leave a scar. I would need thirty to forty stitches.

This is when I woke up. And I woke up the same way I fainted — *screaming*.

They allowed him to hold me, to help hold me steady, to hold my hand. I didn't want to cry but couldn't help it. He wiped my tears.

After it was over I was still a mess, shaking and crying, so they gave me some sort of sedative. He was worried, but they kept telling him not to, that I was just in shock. (*No shit*, I thought to myself. *You'd be in shock too if you saw your blood gushing out of your leg as if it were oil.*) The last thing I remember at the hospital is him leaning over me, kissing me lightly on the lips, and saying, "Everything's all right. You'll be fine. I'm here. I have you. You just rest. I'm going to take you home now."

When I woke up, though, I wasn't at my home; I was at his home, in his bed, my leg propped up on a few pillows. He was seated on the bed's right side, talking to someone. I figured it was my mother when...

"...he was given something to calm him down... No, no, Mrs. Walker, that's not necessary.

He can stay here tonight… No, I don't mind… He shouldn't be moved around much anyway… No, you don't have to worry about that either… No, believe me, it's quite all right. The school will take care of it… Yes, yes, I will have him call you when he wakes up tomorrow morning. He should be out the rest of the night… Yes… It's nothing… Sure… I will… All right… You too… Good-bye."

He hung up the phone. He turned around to face me.

He smiled. "How long you been up?"

"Not long."

He eased onto the bed, placing his left arm around my waist. "So how do you feel?"

"Um…it hurts."

"Well, it will for a little while longer. And you'll have to be off your feet for a week or so just to make sure it's healed. You hungry?"

I shook my head no. I looked deep into his eyes. He frowned.

"What?" he asked.

"I…I'm just happy."

"*Happy?*"

"Just happy you were there. Thank you."

"Anytime, Babe. Anytime."

He bent his body so that I could hold him. I squeezed him as if it were the last time.

"It's all right, Babe. It's all right," he whispered.

"Thank you," I whispered back.

"Anytime, Babe. Anytime."

Pause.

"Don't *ever* give me a scare like that again, you hear?" he demanded. "You know you shouldn't be working on equipment you haven't been trained on, even if it's just for fun."

"Yes. I hear. I know. I'm sorry for scaring you."

"I know. Remember that I love you."

WHOA!

Now, I knew I heard it, but I wanted to hear it again. I mean, it is the type of thing you *like* to hear over and over and over again.

"What did you say?" I asked, anticipating.

"I love you," he repeated, kissing my forehead.

"I...love...you." I said it slowly — not because I wasn't sure of how I felt (hell, I had been waiting to tell him the very first day we met; it was first sight for me). It was because I wanted to hear it come out of my mouth, for as crazy as it sounds, I never really thought I would hear myself say it to anyone. And I *loved* the way it sounded. I fell asleep in his arms, safe and secure in the knowledge that I was

indeed in the arms of the man I loved — and
that *he* loved *me*.

Of course, saying it is one thing; showing it is
another. He had shown it that day by, yes, res-
cuing me. But I found the ultimate proof two
months later in my locker.

I had opened it as I had many times before,
without a second thought; this time I was swap-
ping my journalism workbook for this week's
reading material in literature class: *Night* by
Elie Wiesel. I closed the locker — and did a
double take. I opened it back up and saw what
I thought I saw: a small square red envelope.

Now, I had seen this scene played out before:
Girl opens up locker, girl screams or squeals
with glee upon finding flowers, candy, and/or a
note of some kind from a secret admirer or
boyfriend, who sneaks up behind her. She says
thanks, he says you're welcome, they hug and
kiss, and another love connection has been
signed, sealed, and delivered.

I always wanted it to happen to me but never
thought it would.

I held up the envelope — nothing was written or typed on its front or back — and did a
triple take: I missed the red rose enclosed in a
plastic case, standing up against the locker's

back wall. I looked around. No one was in sight because the next period had already begun. But I wanted this to last; I knew it would be worth being late for.

I lifted up the case, opened it, and smelled the rose. It smelled like…well, like a rose. But this time its ordinary smell was different because it was *my* rose. I inhaled and exhaled very deeply. I closed the case and put it back in the locker. I unsealed the envelope, took out the heart-shaped card, and *gasped:*

TO MY LOVE, WITH ALL MY HEART

Babe:

It's not Valentine's Day
But it doesn't have to be
To tell you in this special way
Just how much you mean to me

As Gladys & The Pips would say:
"You're #1 in My Book"

I LOVE YOU… W.A.R.

I was surprised. I was speechless. I was *stunned.*

127

Getting a Valentine's Day card in November was *so* romantic, *so* sweet, *so* touching, I *had* to shed a few tears.

I placed the card in its envelope and left it in the locker but took the rose to class. I decided that the rest of the school should see what I received. I couldn't say *who* gave it to me, but my knowing would be enough satisfaction.

I was convinced that he loved me. And why wouldn't I be? It was there in black and white (and red).

But as his signature foreshadowed, I was about to be drafted into a W.A.R. — a war in which my emotions, my heart, and my love would be attacked.

I would survive — but not without battle scars.

The End of a Love Affair

They say love is blind. Well, sometimes it can be blind, deaf, dumb, *and* numbing.

Mr. Reid was my life. There was nothing he wanted to do that I didn't want to do. There was nothing I wouldn't do *for* him. And there was nothing he could do *or* say, in my eyes, that was wrong (or so I thought).

For some, what we had was *the* ideal relationship: being with someone who is really a some*thing*, an object, clay to be formed and fitted in any way one wishes, in any place one wishes, for any purpose one wishes. And for over a year this is what Mr. Reid had in me.

But I guess that in the end it felt too good to be loved so bad. While I was under the impression that things were going great between us, he started to drop me hints — indisputable clues — that they weren't.

Everything started to change between us after I won the state championships at the end of March. My training sessions became even more rigorous, for we wanted to be ready for whatever shade the judges would attempt to throw our way. Tuesday morning, Friday evening, and Saturday afternoon were the times I got busy on the equipment — and then *we* got busy. My homohormones, though, would surge on Wednesday, more than likely because our sex-sion on Tuesday was brief (fifteen minutes wasn't long enough to do all the things we liked to do, and that was usually all the time we had since we both had to make our first class).

On one of these very frustrating Wednesdays, I decided I just couldn't wait until the end of the week. I left a note for Mr. Reid on his desk during my lunch break so I could get some after school. No one would see it but him, since I was the only one who had a key to his office (I was mistaken). If our meeting was okay (and why wouldn't it be, since he had never passed on some of *this* before), I told him to leave his desk light on (he always turned all his lights off when he wasn't there, even if he would be gone for a few minutes; he was concerned about saving energy). You can imagine how happy I was when, at the end of the day, I ducked into the phys ed department, opened his door, and found the letter missing and the light on. I turned it off and made my way up to the fifth floor.

To my surprise the doors to the stairwell and gym were unlocked. That was odd: He *always* locked both, just in case someone wandered upstairs who shouldn't have. That should have been a clear sign to me that something was up.

Those faint, hushed grunts and sighs sounded very familiar, and I recognized one of the voices. The other I didn't, and one thing was certain — it wasn't mine.

I stood there, just outside the door, contemplating whether to peek or just leave. I didn't want to believe what I was hearing, and I really didn't want to see it, because seeing *would* be believing. But I did.

There was Mr. Reid, straddled on the pommel horse, as Randall Richardson, the school jock, held on to the horse's handles, rocking and rowing Mr. Reid's boat.

I was *horrified* — and, if the absolute truth be known, turned on — by this sight. It was all

so intense: The man I loved was fucking someone else, and it made me angry, yet watching
other people do what I had come to love doing
so much was...*thrilling* (at that time I didn't
know there was such a thing as an X-rated all-
male video). And let's add that the other person
was a tasty morsel himself: five-ten, 190
pounds, with pretty, dark brown skin and a
booty so round and big that I now knew why he
was known as "wide-receivin' Randy" (being a
great football player had *nothing* to do with it).

And *this* is gonna sound weird, but I felt as
if I were outside of myself, watching myself get
it on with Mr. Reid. Although the body I was
watching was not mine, it was happening in
the same time, same place, and same position,
with the same movement, same heat, and same
passion.

I was almost tempted to pull out my dick
(which was pointing at them with anticipation)
and beat it, but then Mr. Reid moaned...

"Oh, yeah, Babe!"

...and my dick went soft — just *dropped*, you
hear me? — and I didn't hear anything else he
said. All I heard was the sound of my heart —
breaking — as I ran down the stairs, out of the
building, and straight home.

132

Now, any other fool would've known that now was the time to, if not let go, reevaluate what we had. But I wasn't just any other fool — I was a stone-cold fool in love. Despite the evidence that I wasn't the only "Babe," I managed to convince myself that no one could love him like I could, no matter what he thought and no matter who else he decided to have. How could he *not* want me after all we had been through? Yeah, this was definitely my ego talking, something I didn't even know I had until then, and it pushed me to do something that I would never do again — fight for my man. He would come back to me, he would come back for me, and he would *cum* for me again the way he told me, on more than one occasion, he had never done before.

And he did. That Friday I reclaimed my place on the horse and *his* horse, and I had him screaming for me to stop (no, I didn't). My goal was to lay it on him so good that he would see that *I* was all he needed. I was going to prove that I was the mature one — I was a year older than Randy and wasn't about to make myself look stupid by confronting him or Mr. Reid, for I knew I would probably lose it (it wasn't easy — especially when the following week I found them *again*, this time gettin' busy in the bleachers).

But confronting him, I later realized, is *exactly* what Mr. Reid wanted me to do. He was trying to push me to the edge, push me over the ledge, so that I would push him out of my life. I mean, if finding the love of your life entangled with someone else — *twice* — won't do it, what will?

Well, he had a few other tricks in his bag, and they were even more cruel. A week before the finals, I was practicing my (what else?) pommel horse routine, and my dismount was a little off. Well, according to him, it was more than a little off.

"What are you doing?" he demanded to know.

"Hunh?"

"You heard me. What are you doing?"

He had never talked to me this way before — abrupt, harsh, indifferent — and it startled me. "I, uh, I know, uh, I'm somewhat off-center."

He put his hands on his hips. *"Somewhat?* No, you *are* off-center. Let's get it right, okay?" He stared as I climbed back on top. Everything was perfect — except the dismount again.

I decided to beat him to the critical punch. I laughed. "I guess it's not my day."

"Well, you *better* make it your day. That dismount is in*cred*ibly sloppy. You expect to win a national title performing like *that?"*

134

I didn't think it was a question that needed an answer; of course the reply would be no. But he wanted to hear it.

"I'm *talkin'* to you," he huffed. He was now standing over me, his face distorted, his eyes full of contempt.

I was at a loss for words. "I...uh, I, uh, no—"

"Then I suggest you get your *ass* back up there and do it right."

I drew back (well, in) a deep breath, lowered my head, and did as I was told. He got down on one knee in front of the horse. I did the routine again, praying the landing would come off right. It didn't.

He shook his head, flustered. "No, no, *no.*" He clapped his hands. "Do it again."

And I did it again. And again. And again, as he badgered and badgered and badgered me. I had never seen him like this. He was a stern counselor but very sensitive and patient. When I couldn't get something, he always encouraged me, convinced me I could do it. Becoming hostile and making me feel guilty about not performing a move correctly was not his style.

By the time I had mounted the horse for the tenth time, I was crying. But I received no sympathy from him.

"Give me a break, Crawford. You should be able to do this in your sleep. Stop acting like a sissy."

Stop acting like a sissy.

If you're a gay male, I'm sure you can vividly recall hearing that word more times than you can count or than you would care to remember. I'm no exception. It hurt to hear it when I was growing up. It burned. It stung. It scarred. It made me feel less than male, less than boy, less *than*. But what else could I expect from emotionally deficient, sexually insecure delinquents who felt the only way to feel better about themselves was to question the sexuality, the manhood, the *person*hood of others?

I never expected, I never thought I would hear it from a man I respected. A man I admired. A man I looked up to.

The man I loved.

It didn't just hurt when he said it; it *pained*. It pained me so much that I climbed atop that horse, worked my body with a vengeance, and landed on point.

I didn't wait for his reaction — I sprinted out of the gym to the locker room, where I really broke down.

He didn't come after me, and I'm glad he didn't; I wouldn't want to hear anything he had to say, nor would I have had anything to say to him. I continued to cry, steaming as the steam filled the shower room. I must have been in there for a half hour.

As I was coming out, he stood before me naked. I attempted to walk past him, but he blocked my path. I pushed forward; he pushed me back and into the room. I pulled him away from me; he pulled me toward him. I fought him; he fought me back. He forced me to kiss him — and just like before, everything worked itself out (this time, though, we staked out the wet, cool tile floor). While he didn't *say* "I'm sorry," he did *show* it.

But at least in that case he showed it. He had no remorse or regret the other times.

I finished in eighth place in the nationals, which were held in D.C. (my first and certainly not my last trip to Chocolate City). I was the first African-American to make the top ten and the only student from the East Coast (the top three were from the West, with three each also coming from the Midwest and the South). I played the game well: always smiling for the cameras, always being available to the press, always appearing humble and gracious to the judges. And I'm sure the selection we chose for my floor

performance — Lionel Richie's "Hello" — also
made a difference (he was "safer" than Stevie
Wonder). My showing was no small accom-
plishment, considering all the emotional stress I
was under. Not only was Mr. Reid distant (he
didn't say a word on the drive down or back to
New York), but he was also holding back — we
hadn't had sex in several weeks (and the proof
we weren't was beginning to show: My acne,
which had all but disappeared after we started
kickin' it, was making a return engagement).
Every time I pushed up, he pulled back.

We stayed in our separate rooms on the D.C.
trip, and he wasn't interested in having company
the following weekend to celebrate my triumph (I
just *knew* this would force him to get up off his
high horse and get up off that lovin' — I mean,
this is what we had been working so hard to
achieve — but I was more excited about my successful showing than he was). I figured Randy
was beating my time but still played it cool and
beat *my* time, knowing that he would, once again,
come to his senses and come on back.

Then, the day after Memorial Day, we were
sitting in his office, looking at a few of the arti-
cles in the national media that featured me in
their finals coverage, when...

"Are you going to the prom?" he asked, not looking up from one of the newspapers.

While there were a few female students who expressed interest in being my date (most of them, I'm sure, because of my high-profile status as a national athletic champion), I wasn't the least bit interested in attending or in them. As far as I was concerned, it didn't prove any point to play that straight role that one night since I didn't my entire high school career. So my answer was a casual...

"No."

"Well..." His voice trailed off; he was hesitating. "Uh...how would you like to have our own prom?"

"Our...own prom?"

"Yes. We can go out...to dinner. And dancing."

"Dancing?"

"Yes, dancing."

"You...and me?"

"Yes, you and me," he laughed, that playful part of the old him shining through. He finally looked up. "You and me."

Mind you, I didn't even know there was such a thing as a gay bar or club, so I asked...

"But...where can *we* go dancing?"

"Oh, there are a lot of places. Ha, most of them *you* can't get into. But I'm sure we can find one."

I was shocked by the invitation — not to mention that this was the very first cordial exchange we had had in some time.

"When do you want to go?" I asked.

"When else? Prom night should be a special night — even if you don't go to the prom." He smiled. "Is it a date?"

I smiled too and could feel those homo-hormones kick in gear. "Yes."

But I should've known I was once again being set up to be let down.

My mother was so happy I had decided to go to the prom that she was willing to accept my explanation for going solo: With so many young ladies to choose from, I didn't want to break anyone's heart (our school didn't require that you have a date). Since my Uncle Russ was in town from Chicago on business and was staying at the Marriott in midtown, my transportation to the prom was taken care of (he gave me cab fare to get to his hotel when it was over; I would stay with him, and we'd hook up with the rest of the family late Saturday).

But after he dropped me off at Tavern on the Green, I hopped the train and headed for Penn

Station before any of my classmates noticed me. I stood in front of Madison Square Garden, very much out of place in a black tuxedo, which I had rented with my own money. The Harlem Globetrotters were performing that evening, and some of the fans (even the women) came dressed in basketball tanks and shorts, as if they would be challenging the original G's themselves.

Nine o'clock came, the time he decided on. No Mr. Reid.

Nine-fifteen. *He must be stuck in traffic,* I thought to myself.

Nine-thirty. *Hmm. I hope he didn't have an accident or something.*

Nine forty-five. *Where could he be?*

By the time 10 o'clock rolled around, I was hungry and cold (while the mercury hovered around sixty, it was rather windy). I was also tired of being hit on, although a few of the pick-up lines were clever ("You lookin' mighty clean there, little man. How 'bout you and me gettin' dirty together?"). I circled the entire block, searching for him, making sure I didn't get the directions mixed up and he wasn't waiting for me in another area around the Garden.

At 10:10 I called him. After three rings the phone picked up.

"Hello?" It was him.

"Mr. Reid?"

"Mitchell?" Uh-huh...Mitchell. That was another thing that had changed. The last time he called me "Babe" was when we had made love in the locker room. He seemed surprised to hear my voice — and that made me a little annoyed.

"Yes, it's me," I said with a *who else would it be?* tone.

"Hmm, it's after 10. Why are you calling at this hour?"

Why am I calling at this hour?

For him every night was a school night, which meant lights were out at 9:45 — that is, unless we were busy doing other things.

"What happened to you?" I demanded. "I've been *waiting* for over an hour."

"*Waiting* for over an hour? Waiting for what?"

Waiting for what? He's *got* to be kidding.

I became very flustered. "Waiting for *you*. I'm at Madison Square Garden. We're supposed to go out tonight. You're my prom date, remember?"

Silence.

He sighed real heavy. "Oh, Mitchell, I forgot. I...something came up, and—"

"Something came up? What could've—"

"I…I can't talk about it right now. I've got to go. I…I'll see you at school."

Click.

Ker-plunk, ker-plunk, ker-plunk went my heart again.

I was what they would call in the dating world stood up. But this wasn't just any old date. Being dissed on prom night has to rank right up there with being left at the altar. I wanted to call him back and curse his ass out but didn't. And I wanted to cry but forced myself not to (it wasn't easy). I just took the twenty dollars my mother gave me in case of an emergency and treated myself to dinner at Beefsteak Charlie's. Even though he shouldn't have, the waiter allowed me to have a quarter glass of wine (turned out he was a big gymnastics fan and recognized me).

I hung out in the lobby of the Marriott until 1 o'clock (I'm sure that if I had been wearing a pair of jeans and sneakers, the hotel personnel would have asked me to leave). While I did my best to make it appear I had a great time, Uncle Russ could see right through my act. He said I could talk to him about it, but…well, *what* could I say: that I've been having an affair with

my gymnastics coach for over a year, things
have turned sour, and tonight he pounded yet
another nail in the coffin of our love? I didn't
think he would tell my mother; I had confided
in him many times about many things. But this
was different from playing hooky from school
in the eighth grade. Disclosing the affair
would've forced me to disclose and confront
myself (I would learn several years later that
Uncle Russ was also attempting to confront
himself).

Instead of a pep talk, he gave me something
I *really* needed. I hadn't touched or been
touched by a man in two months, and having
his warm, hard body pressed against mine and
strong arms around me fit the bill. In fact, I had
to catch myself: As far as my dick was concerned, it didn't matter that this man was my
uncle, but I managed to keep it under control.
(The same could *not* be said for Uncle Russ: I
had never noticed how big he was until I was
poked several times during the night in the
belly, waist, and leg. Not even the sweatpants
he wore could camouflage it.)

That Monday was my graduation, and while
Mr. Reid was there, he made himself invisible.
He was nowhere to be found after the ceremo-

ny. Being the lovesick puppy I was, I called him every day the rest of that week; of course, there was no response.

On Saturday my mother had a special barbecue at Aunt Ruth's to celebrate my getting my diploma and winning a four-year scholarship to St. John's University in Queens. I called Mr. Reid that morning, reminding him that he was invited, and left the directions, knowing full well he wasn't going to show. He didn't let me down.

I decided not to call him Sunday; that would surely surprise him. But then *he* surprised *me:* On Monday evening I dialed his number and was shocked when a recording announced, "I'm sorry. The number you have dialed has been changed. No further information is available."

He changed his number? Oh, no, *that* was the straw.

The next day I made that very long trek to his home by bus and train (I would have to get used to this particular ride, since he lived but a mile from my college). It was early enough in the day before the first doorman came on duty, so I was able to slip in when someone came out.

I got to his door. I rang the bell. I knocked. No answer.

I rang it again and knocked harder. No answer.

I began to walk away, when I heard the peep-hole click. I turned back and banged on the door.

"Mr. Reid? Mr. Reid, are you there?"

No answer.

"Please, I have to talk to you. Please, open up."

No answer.

"I...I know you're in there. Please, I just need to talk to you."

Still no answer.

Okay, I thought, *two can play this game.* He would have to leave the apartment sometime, and I was determined to wait. The lobby was out: The security guard would be arriving any minute. I couldn't wait by his door or hang out on the floor, for someone might get suspicious. So I ducked into the stairwell directly across from his apartment.

For two hours I stood inside the stairwell. Finally I heard something, but it wasn't a key rattling or a door unlocking. Someone had gotten off the elevator and was walking my way. He stopped in front of the door.

I'd recognize that back anywhere.

I emerged from the stairwell. "Mr. Reid?"

He froze. I waited for him to turn to face me. He wouldn't.

I was shaking. My voice was cracking. "Please...please talk to me."

He still wouldn't move. He didn't speak.

"I...I..." I was searching. I found the words. "I thought you loved me."

Now, this moment in my life, I will never forget, even though I wish I could. He turned around — in slow motion. The look on his face said it all.

Uh-oh. Ooh-ooh. Look out. Here it comes.

His face was blank; he looked past me. "I never loved you. How could I? You're just a kid. You're not my student anymore. Don't come around again. Good-bye."

And then he went inside his apartment and officially closed the door on me and on us.

I guess I could have screamed, hollered, prevented him from going in, tried to force my way in, slapped, punched, kicked, spit, basically gone crazy — you know, all the melodramatic things you're supposed to do when you've been rejected. Given all the shit he put me through, I would've had every right to fuck with him and fuck him over like he did me. But I took the

147

high road: I didn't follow the psychotic lead of
Jessica Walter in *Play Misty for Me* or get my
ass up on my shoulders, shouting, *"And I am
telling you, I'm not going."* He was telling me
good-bye for months, but I refused to heed the
warnings. Hearing it from his own mouth
signed it and sealed it.

The masquerade was over...and so was love.

So there were no tears; I had cried enough. I
walked away defeated but decided to stick
around. I didn't want to see him; I wanted to
see the other reason why I was dismissed. The
reason he didn't mention. The reason that was
waiting for him inside his apartment. And I did.

He and wide-receivin' Randy hopped in his
car ten minutes later.

Yet I knew that there was more to our love
affair's ending than what I saw or what he
expressed. But I never thought I'd see the day
when I'd have the chance to find out.

But now that day — or, rather, that night —
had come.

Back 2 the Present Time…

After I recounted this whole sordid tale to B.D. over a plate of bacon, grits, and eggs at the Pink Tea Cup in the Vill, he argued that no matter how much I may have hated Mr. Reid for what he did and no matter how much I may still hate him, *hate* wouldn't be what I would be feeling when I saw him again after so many years. Those feelings I believed were no longer there would sneak back up on me, and I might find myself wanting to *feel* something with him again.

Of course I protested. "That's ridiculous."

"What's so ridiculous about it?"

"Well, I am in love with and love another man, remember?"

"So?"

"So?"

"That's right, so? There is no question that you love and you're in love with Pooquie. But that ain't got nothin' to do with what went down a decade ago."

"How you figure?"

"Look, you are *beginning* to build a history with Pooquie. You already *have* a history with this man — a history that, might I add, has *not* been resolved."

"What do you mean?"

He gave me one of those *You trippin'* looks. "Are you sure that *I'm* the dense one in this family?"

We laughed.

"There is a lot of unfinished *biz*ness there — things to say…things to do. I mean, we're talking about your first love. And as Miki Howard once cooed, there *is* such a thing as a new fire from an old flame."

"I don't feel a fire for him—"

"How would you know if you do or don't? You're not gonna know until the moment you lay eyes on him again. While the love may be lost, the longing, the lust *never* goes away. It's gonna be hard, *very* hard, to just ignore it — *especially* when he is so p-h-y-n-e."

"He might not be anymore."

He grinned. "Ha, is that wishful thinking?"

I grinned too.

"Honey, listen, good Black don't crack, all right? *We* just don't age gracefully; we age *gorgeously*. Ain't nothin' sexier than a Black man with salt-and-pepper hair and a beard. Oof, Lord! Imagine what *Babyface* will look like in ten, twenty years. *Chile*, as his wife, I look forward to *that!*"

We cracked up.

He kept on schoolin' me. "He *might* have a little gray, and that ain't your cup of cappuccino. He *might* have added pounds in *all* the wrong places. And he *might* have a wrinkle or two — or two *hundred*. But believe me, when you see him, it'll be like time has stood still: You'll be looking into the eyes of the man you *used* to love, *not* the man standing in front of you. You'll be seeing a man who isn't ten years older but ten years *younger*."

Well, as is often the case when it comes to men, B.D. was right. The package in front of me had changed some — he added some more bulk to his physique (which was being hugged quite nicely by the short-sleeved mud cloth shirt and black slacks he wore), while the cir-

cles under his eyes and the patch of gray hair
near his left temple gave away his true age —
but it didn't matter. Seeing him after so long, I
felt a rush. When I looked into his eyes, it
seemed as if time had not marched on, that it
was still 1984, not 1994.

And as we took each other in, the first Negro
selection of the evening came on (which was
released a year *before* I began high school):
"Reunited" by Peaches & Herb.

He caught the irony too. "Mmm-hmm…and
it feels so good." He smiled.

I really didn't want to smile, but I did too.
"Does it?"

"Of course it does. I dreamed about this day
a lot."

"You have?"

"Yes. And you look even better than I could
have dreamed."

Uh-huh, he still knew what to say.

But instead of thanking him for the compliment, I flung it back at him with some shade.
"Well, I wish I could say the same."

"Excuse me?"

"I wish I could also say that I had dreamed
about this day."

"You haven't?"

"No."

"Why is that?"

Is he serious? He knows why not. But I played along.

"Well, I was given a very good reason not to dream about this reunion or you. Remember?"

Yeah, he remembered. He stroked his clean-shaven chin. "You mean to tell me that you have not dreamed about me at all, not even once after all these years?"

"No," I lied.

He bent his body forward, grinning. "But you *have* thought about me...?"

I decided to give him this one. "Yes, I have."

"Good things, I hope...?"

"Maybe...maybe not."

"Well, I hope to find out about those things and everything else that's been going on in your life later tonight."

My heart began to skip. "Later...tonight?"

"Yes. We'll head out afterward for a drink and—" he leaned in closer; I could now feel his cool breath against my forehead "—and catch up." He winked.

I knew how he wanted to "catch up," and I had to catch myself: I was feeling weak, I was feeling wet, and I was feeling warm. Yes, some of those old feelings were coming back, and to tell you the truth, the name *Pooquie* was the furthest thing from my mind. And his invitation made me recall B.D.'s warning: "Don't go out for a cocktail or you may wind up with a cock *up* your tail."

But then...

"*Mitchell Crawford!* There you are! Ah, you have not changed a bit! I have been looking all over for you. Now, the program is about to begin, and we need you up on stage right this minute..."

It was "Our Miss Brooks" — Beverly Brooks, the school's activities director. She looks *nothing* like Eve Arden, the star of that '50s TV series. She favors Zelda Rubinstein, who schooled us about "the light" in *Poltergeist* (take away the glasses and add a platinum beehive do and that trademark blood-red shawl she wears no matter the season). She has been planning all Murrow functions since the school opened twenty years ago — graduations, freshman orientations, dances, proms, concerts, theatrical productions, cultural events, job fairs, even going-away bashes for faculty. You have to be patient and pushy to do such a job, and like Ms. Zelda, Our Miss Brooks is a little lady with a lot of zest. She gets the job done and then some.

I *needed* to be rescued, so she was whisking me off at just the right time. She grabbed my right hand and looked up — *way up* — at Mr. Reid. "Oh, please excuse us, Warren. You two will have a chance to catch up later on."

"Yes, we will," he responded, grinning as we left.

As we made our way to the stage, the music stopped and Mr. Leonardo stepped up to the mike. "Ladies and gentlemen, may I have your attention." By the time we were both seated, he continued, welcoming everyone back. He then turned things over to Our Miss Brooks, who proceeded to reintroduce the stars of the past: the king and queen of the prom, the most popular boy and girl, the prettiest girl, the most handsome boy, the best-dressed boy and girl, the student with the best personality, the student most likely to succeed...

And then it was my turn.

"And now we will have a few words from our class valedictorian, Mitchell Crawford."

I thanked her and forgot all about the typed statement I had tucked in my shirt pocket. Pooquie and Junior helped me with it.

"Good evening. It's hard to believe that ten years have passed. And what a ten years it has been! A *lot* has happened since we last saw each other. The world has definitely changed. The Berlin Wall has fallen. The Cold War is over. Nelson Mandela is free. The stock market crashed again. Crack cocaine and AIDS have devastated us. Oprah has enlightened us. Roseanne has entertained us. We can reach out and touch by fax or the Internet. And there's a Democrat in the White House!"

They laughed.

"And look at us. Like the world, we have also been transformed. We have also evolved. We have grown. But it's a different transformation, a different evolution, a different type of growth. As the world has spun, we have been seeking our place in it, the meaning of it, the meaning of life, the meaning of our *own* lives. And as we enter our trying — or is it turbulent? — thirties, it's only fitting that we come back to the place where it all began. This is where we began to seek, where we began to search, where we began to dream. I hope that your search was a pleasurable one — not too many bumps or lumps along the way — and you got ahold of those dreams. And if you haven't, remember:

It's never too late to start. Let tonight be a
reminder, a symbol of not just where we've
been but where we still have to go. Good luck,
God bless, and good night." I shook Mr.
Leonardo's hand and hugged Miss Brooks
before I left the stage.

Avery Sumpter was the final act on the bill.
This brother loved Michael Jackson so much
that he wore that trademark Sgt. Pepper com-
modore's coat and white sequined glove every
day. *Everyone* — students, teachers, faculty, the
principal, even the custodial staff — knew it
was a mistake to even mention you-know-who's
name in his presence, especially if what you had
to say wasn't nice. He took any criticism as a
personal attack on him and would defend
Michael's honor (and his ego) to the death (he
was suspended from school for two days for
slugging someone who questioned Michael's talent). He could talk about Michael all day, and
since Michael was everywhere in our junior and
senior years, Avery always had a new article to
show off, another photo to post on or in his
locker, or new sales figures to report (when
Thriller sold a million copies in one week, he
had a party to celebrate, and when Michael had
that accident while filming the Pepsi commer-

cial, he wore a ribbon similar to the one folks
sported in memory of the two dozen Black males
killed in Atlanta). But thank God he didn't carry
his obsession *too* far: He still had the rich dark
skin, big broad nose, thick lips, and uncleft double chin he was born with.

That Jackson jacket still fit, but he decided to
do without the glove this evening. He stepped
up to the mike, looked straight ahead, closed
his eyes, and nodded. The lights went down, a
spotlight fell on him, and a projector clicked on.
He began singing "Gone Too Soon" as Our Miss
Brooks joined him on the piano and the yearbook photos of our classmates who were *gone
too soon* flashed on a screen.

Keith Cathcart. He was a rich white kid
from Sheepshead Bay. How rich was he? He
was driven to and from school by his *own*
chauffeur and valet, an elderly Black man he
called Hoke (uh-huh, Driving *Mr.* Daisy). His
wardrobe consisted of cardigans and sports
jackets, Kenneth Cole shoes and London Fog
coats. And, yes, he "talked" like he had dollars: He would speak with an "air" (you know,
head tilted slightly upward and to the side,
eyebrows raised) and often said things like "My
word," "How quaint," and "Surely you jest"

(no, he wasn't British). I noticed, though, how he never smiled, leaving me to believe that he wasn't really happy. It's a cliché, but it's true: Money might buy you a lot of pleasure in this life, but it *can't* buy you happiness. He must have come to the same conclusion: After dropping out of three different colleges in three years, he shot himself in the head on his twenty-first birthday.

Pauline "Paul" Petrillo. Yes, she was called Paul, and she didn't mind at all. She put the *tom* in *tomboy* (Jo Polniaczek on *The Facts of Life* had nothin' on her) and won the other medal for excellence in physical and health education on graduation day (yours truly took the other). In fact, that day, like every other, she wore her Doc Martens (you just *know* Our Miss Brooks gagged). At least she retired the leather jacket and ripped jeans for a few hours for a casual pantsuit. She also refrained from smoking but didn't give up puffin' a pack a day (she apparently started at twelve). She was one of the 65,000 people who died of lung cancer in 1992. Of course, who she left behind surprised many folks: a husband of five years and four-year-old twin girls. Most folks assumed she was a lesbian. Either her husband didn't mind or she was yet another example of how the drag one wears isn't always an indication of who or what one is.

Garrett Wilmington. The brother was a giant — six-four and way over 250 pounds — but was the most withdrawn, shy, quiet student in the whole school. Even Norm the Nerd had more bite than he did. Garrett and Adam became friends (and why not, since Adam was somewhat of a giant himself, reaching the six-foot mark at thirteen), but they lost contact when Adam left New York to attend classes at Florida A&M. A routine traffic stop at 2 A.M. ended Garrett's life at twenty-four. The police alleged that "he wouldn't comply with repeated requests to keep his hands where they could be seen" (someone is pointing a loaded gun at your face and you're not going to comply?), "was verbally abusive" (uh-huh...I'm sure *he* wasn't the one talking out of the side of his neck), "became uncontrollably violent" (of course, it's in our genes, right?), "struck an officer" (if he did — and, knowing Garrett, he didn't — I'm sure it was self-defense), "resisted arrest" (how can he resist arrest when one officer is clubbing him, another is kicking him, and yet another is cutting off his oxygen supply with a choke hold?), and "had to be restrained with force" (i.e., killed). Even though a grand jury refused to indict any of the officers (what a surprise), a civil court jury awarded his family $5 million earlier this year. The irony: Garrett was getting his degree at the John Jay College of Criminal Justice in the hopes of becoming a police officer.

Laberta Ellington. Now, this sister had a *voice* on her, a voice that was deep, plush, and way beyond her years. While most students went around hummin' the latest pop hit, she would school the musically illiterate with selections by Ruth Brown, Etta James, and Billie Holiday. She was the first person at Murrow to be accepted into Juilliard, became a *Star Search* champ, and paid her dues by hitting the concert circuit with the likes of Grover Washington Jr., Jonathan Butler, and George Benson. They say she was about to sign her first record deal in 1990 when she was raped and strangled to death in Brooklyn's Prospect Park. Naturally, I didn't know about it because the story didn't get the play it should have — she was the wrong color and got attacked in the wrong place (if she had been white and it had been Central Park, the racist dailies and newscasts would have certainly put out a frantic "wilding" bulletin to capture the culprits). To this day her killers haven't been caught.

Nathan "Natalie" Crosby. "She" was the only openly gay male student at the school — i.e., she knew who she was, was proud of it, and was brave enough to be herself. Of course, some had a problem with her "flaunting her sexuality" and made it known, including Jasper Morris, an overstuffed baked potato of a wrestler who didn't feel that Natalie "presented the right kind of Black male image" (I guess he felt his idol, Mr. T, did: *The A-Team* was, in Jasper's eyes, "the greatest show ever on TV," and he gave the show and its star more publicity by doing his classwork in a Mr. T notebook and purchasing a Mr. T doll). I would see their confrontation at a bus stop many times in different forms in the future: a so-called heterosexual thinks he's gonna teach one of us faggots what being a real man is all about — and *gags.* As Natalie, a mere 140 pounds and no taller than I, tae kwon do'd his 200-plus-pound ass into the pavement, Jasper was screamin', cryin' out, beggin' for mercy, not to mention his mama. It wasn't a surprise to most that Natalie died of AIDS complications. But I think it made several of the men in the room, including

Jasper, pause, since Natalie always made it clear that Jasper and his crew picked on her because "I won't let them put their square pegs in my round hole." Uh-huh…makes you wonder if she did.

Gregory "Peanut" O'Hara. He was called Peanut because that was all he would munch on — before, after, and even during breakfast and lunch. He also had a love for animals — he carried around pictures of his two Siamese cats (Aristotle and Venus), his parakeet (Bunny), his goldfish (Pat), and his dalmatian (Kim). He lobbied the science department to offer a course on endangered species, but they rejected the idea. He became the leader of a group called ARCH (Animal Rights Champions); I recall seeing him on the news one night, picketing a film because it showed a cat being mutilated, and a short profile on him in *People* in which he chastised celebrities for wearing fur. He was killed in a hit-and-run two years ago, but some in the animal rights movement still say his death was not an accident.

Georgia Greenbaum. A petite girl with Shirley Temple locks and braces, she lived but three blocks from the school and was late almost every single day. Why wasn't she put on probation? Suspended? Kicked out? Her father, Ivan, was an assistant superintendent of schools. Daddy always looked out for his little girl, but he apparently didn't know that she was being verbally, mentally, and physically abused by her beau, Hugh Bumgarten — and, boy, oh, boy, was he a *bum*. I had the misfortune of witnessing one of his violent outbursts, slapping her across the face and calling her a bitch. They still got married after she graduated from college, and she continued to hide the bruises and scars. One night he came home drunk, accusing her of cheating on him and claiming the baby she was carrying wasn't his. When she announced that she and her unborn child deserved better and that she was leaving him, he began to beat and kick her. She died after being on a respirator for three weeks, but Faith, her daughter, whom the doctors delivered two months prematurely, survived. Faith is now living with her grandparents, and Hugh is in jail for life (his parental rights have been terminated by the courts, and he can have no contact with Faith). It's a shame that it took her bringing a life into the world for Georgia to see that her own life was worth something and worth saving.

This was indeed a somber, tender moment. Avery finished the last verse in tears as folks pulled out tissues and a few sobbed loudly. Even I cried, and I didn't really have relationships with any of those who died. Our Miss Brooks allowed us all time to collect ourselves before she officially closed out the program.

As soon as the lights came back up, there was Mr. Reid by my (right) side.

"Are you all right?" he asked.

I sighed. "Yes, I'll be fine."

"Hmm, I can already see that." He smiled.

I wasn't amused. I frowned.

"So would you like to leave and have a party of our own?"

Hunh? We just had what amounted to a memorial service, and he's talking about getting him some? How insensitive can he be? I wanted to ask him, but I already knew the answer.

I shrugged. "I guess we can go out for a drink. But I can't be out too late. I have a very important appointment in the morning."

"Don't worry. I'll get you home at a decent hour. But that doesn't mean what we do before then will be decent."

He grinned; I didn't.

"I have to take care of a few things, and I guess you'll want to say good-bye to people. I can meet you outside the school in, say, ten minutes…?"

I felt like sitting in the shade again. "Ten minutes? Sure that's all you'll need? Are you sure you'll be on time? Are you sure you'll show up?"

He knew where I was going. He frowned. "Yes, I'm sure — three times, all right?"

"Okay," I mouthed.

"Good. I have a feeling this is going to be a night to remember."

I shrugged. He nodded and left. I said my good-byes and exchanged numbers with several folks. I went upstairs to the second floor and found my hall locker, #221. It was now painted a bright yellow; I laughed because it reminded me of the Jeep Pooquie wanted to buy. I tried my old combination on the lock. No, it didn't open.

When I got outside, he was standing on the driver's side of his car, the motor running.

"You're late."

"Yes, I know. My good-byes took longer than I thought they would. Besides, it's about time *you* were kept waiting."

"Oh, it is?"

I ignored his inquiry. I gave his green Saab a once-over. "Hmm...so you finally traded in that Bug, hunh?"

He laughed. "Please, years ago. Get in."

I did. "Well, let's see if she's got anything on the Bug."

We buckled up, and he pulled off. He was filling me in on when and how he got his new wheels when I heard someone call him. We stopped at the corner for a red light, and the voice became louder and closer, footsteps running. A young man appeared at the window on the driver's side. I recognized him; he had given out photo tags for my classmates and me to wear. I then noticed that mine was still attached to my blue shirt; I took it off.

He bent down. "Where are you going?" he asked, somewhat out of breath.

"I have to run an errand."

He looked at me and then Warren, puzzled. "Well, you will be back, won't you?"

"Yes, I will," Warren replied without looking at him. He rolled up his window and stepped on the gas.

And it was then that any other lust I felt was lost.

*   *   *

"So what's his name?"

We were sitting at the bar in a nightclub not far from Killaretha's called Pink Flamingo, where First Lady, the resident white drag queen, was butchering the greatest hits of Helen Reddy. I didn't know that such a place existed or that he knew where Greenwich Village was. But several of the patrons (some white, some Black) acknowledged him. I didn't have much to say; I spoke only when he asked a question. I gave him a very condensed and sketchy version of my life over the past ten years, and the only time I became somewhat animated was when I revealed that my next celebrity interview would be with Anita Baker. That touched off a ten-minute debate regarding her best recordings. He reminded me that I first heard her sing dancing in his arms. I think the frown on my face made it clear that it was *not* a fond memory.

He then hoped to engage me in a discussion about another of his favorite artists, someone who came along a year after I graduated — Sade. But I wasn't feeling it. I wanted to know what he had been up to the past decade — or at least the past *few* years. I really didn't have to ask because I saw it (or, rather, him) with my own eyes. But I decided to go there anyway.

Of course, he didn't want to punch the ticket. "Who?"

"*You* know who…the student, at the school, who came after you."

"Oh, him. That's Pierce."

"Pierce. Hmm…"

"What?"

"Oh, oh, nothing."

"*That* was something. Go ahead, say it."

"Well…it's just that…I recognized that look."

"That look?"

"Yes, that look he wore. I bet he's a senior."

"Yes, he is."

"And I bet he's a *champion*."

"Hunh?"

"You know. A future Olympic gold gymnast."

"Ah. Yes, he has a lot of potential to be just that."

"So, uh, how good is he, *ahem*, on the mat?"

He glanced at me, smiling. Yes, motherfucker, I just made a dig at you. He decided to shrug it off. "He happens to be very good."

"I bet. Won any titles?"

"State championships two years running."

"Ah. And how did he place in the nationals?"

"Seventh last year, fourth this year."

"Not bad. I bet you're really proud of him."

"Yes, I am. I…I was proud of you too, you know."

Hmm…now where did *that* come from?
"Uh-huh."

"Uh-huh, what?"

"Uh-huh. Just uh-huh."

"Well, I was. *You* could have been the King of
Barcelona in '92 instead of Vitaly Scherbo." He
expected me to validate his feelings, but I
refused. He sighed, then smiled. "Uh, he's valedictorian, just like you were."

"Oh, really?"

"Yes."

"And I bet he's a HIT, just like I was."

"A HIT?"

"Yes: a Homosexual in Training."

He choked on his drink.

I giggled. "History *does* repeat itself. So, uh,
when will the circle be completed?"

He regained his composure. "A HIT? Circle
be completed? What do you—"

"You know: When are you going to dump
him — as if *I* didn't know?"

"Dump him?"

"Yes, dump him."

He had this look that said, *How dare you suggest
such a thing!* "Do you think that *I*…? And *he*…?"

"I don't *think*. I *know* that *you* and *he*…yes."

"What would make you think that?"

"One, I know you. Two, it was written all over his face. And three, I was there…uh…how long has it been? Oh, yes, a decade ago."

"Wait, wait, let's back up for a minute here: You *know* me?"

"Yes."

"You haven't seen me in ten years, so how would you *know* me?"

"Okay, let's put it this way: I know *about* you, and I *know* what you like."

"*Do* you now?" He moved in closer, putting his left arm around my stool. He grinned. "And what *do* I like?"

"Hmm, let's see. I can see the ad right now: 'Black male, fifteen to seventeen years of age, under five feet nine inches, 125 to 140 pounds, compact and cute, wanted by "coach" to learn *all* the right moves. I'll show you the way to touch and get *in* touch with your body.' Does that about sum it up?"

"Oh, I see. Are you talking about Pierce, or are you talking about *you*?"

I folded my arms across my chest. "Are you actually sitting there *denying* that you and Pierce are involved?"

"No, I'm not denying that we're involved. I am his coach, and he is my student."

171

"Uh-huh, in more ways than one," I whispered under my breath.

"What did you say?"

"Nothing, nothing... Well, it would be a waste of time telling you not to hurt him because I know you already have."

"Hurt him? What makes you think that?"

"Uh, I've taken that trip already, remember?"

He shrugged.

I sighed. "This is gonna sound...I don't know, silly, crazy. But I want you to promise me something."

"Promise you something? What?"

I took a deep breath. "Don't make him think it's his fault."

"What?"

"Make sure he knows that it's not something that he said...that it's not something that he did...that he knows it's not about *him*."

He was still in denial; what an asshole. "Look, I'm sure you didn't come here to talk about Pierce."

"No...no, I didn't. But I just don't want Pierce to be sitting here ten years from now."

"What do you mean?"

"You know just what the *fuck* I mean, *Adolphus*."

He was really thrown for a loop. I had never cursed in his presence before, nor had I ever addressed him in any way except "Mr. Reid." And just like me, he hated his middle name.

"*Adolphus?*" he repeated, flabbergasted. "You are really goin' for your guns, aren't you?"

"Well, when one messes with people's lives the way you have, he shouldn't leave home without wearing a bulletproof vest."

"Babe, why—"

"*Babe?* After all you put me through, you have the unmitigated gall to sit there and call me *Babe?* I bet you call *him* that too, hunh?"

My voice grew a little louder, and a few people turned to look. He nervously smiled in their direction and then returned to me. "Look. Maybe...maybe we should leave and go someplace else to talk—"

"Uh-huh, like your apartment, right?"

"I...I just don't understand why you are being so cold and bitter."

"I don't believe I am being cold or bitter. But if I *were*, I would have good reason to be."

He placed his elbows on the edge of the bar and folded his arms. "All right, all right. I can see that...some of us still live in the past."

"Excuse me?"

"Well, it's obvious that you've held a grudge all these years because I...because I—"

"—*dumped me?*"

"I didn't dump you."

"You didn't? What would *you* call it, then?"

"It...it was a mistake."

"*What* was a mistake?"

"You...and I...being together."

"Was it? Why?"

"You know why."

"Uh...yes, I guess I do. Your mistake was lying to me."

"Lying to you?"

"Yes. Telling me that you loved me."

"I wasn't lying to you when I said that. I really did love you."

"Hmm...why don't I believe that?"

"You don't have to believe it. I *did* love you."

"Uh-huh. Isn't it amazing how one can turn that emotion off as soon as the person they are allegedly in love with is no longer at their disposal?"

"Hunh?"

"I mean, wasn't it rather convenient of you to fall *out* of love with me when I was about to graduate?"

"I didn't fall *out* of love with you. It's just that...we weren't ready for it."

"*We?*"

"Yes."

"You and I weren't ready? *What,* pray say, were we *not* ready for?"

"We...we were in too deep. We...I shouldn't have...it was a mistake."

"I see...so instead of admitting that *it* was all a mistake, that we *were* in too deep and we shouldn't have gotten involved in the first place, and that it wouldn't be a good idea for us to see each other anymore even though you *claim* you still loved me, you tell me that you were never really in love with me because I was just a kid, that I was just your student and there could never be anything that serious between us, right?"

He frowned. "You just have all the answers, don't you?"

I sipped my drink. "If you say I do, I guess I do."

He clapped, then clasped his hands. "What...what do you want me to say? That I'm sorry? That I didn't mean to hurt you? That I felt terrible about the way things had to be?"

"No. I wouldn't want you to say any of those things, because you wouldn't mean them."

He stared me down. "How the *fuck* would you know?"

The few folks around us gazed again. This time all eyes were on me, waiting for my comeback. For those that could hear me, they weren't disappointed.

"*If* you were that sorry about what happened, *if* you didn't mean to hurt me, and *if* you really felt that bad about the way things supposedly had to be, then I wouldn't be hearing this ten years later, now would I?"

He sat back in his stool, looking up.

"It didn't matter to you that my world crashed. And it's not gonna matter when Pierce's does in a few weeks."

"Will you just leave him out of this—"

"*He* is very much a part of this."

A slight grin formed across his face. "Are you jealous?"

"Jealous?" I laughed. "Now, *that's* a good one."

"Well, are you?"

"How could I be jealous of a teenager who, after being brainwashed to believe that he is needed, he is wanted, he is loved, he *is* love, is about to be robbed of his faith, not to mention his innocence and self-worth?" I smiled at him. "Oh, yeah, I am jealous."

"Pierce is *not* you."

"No, he isn't. But he *is* a carbon copy of me, and it makes one wonder how many others came before me, came after me, and will come after him."

He shook his head in disbelief. "I just can't believe this. Now I am really insulted."

"Are you? About what?"

"Do you *really* believe that I make a habit of sleeping with my students?"

"Stu*dents*. That can be two or twenty. Either way, it's a fact. But I'll give you the benefit of the doubt: Let's say I was first. What number is Pierce? Certainly not number two."

"He *isn't* a number two, and even if he were, that's none of your business."

"Well, he would at least be number three. After all, we can't forget Randy."

"Randy?"

"Uh-huh, Randy. I'm sure *he'll* be sitting here next year, querying you about me, and you will once again develop amnesia."

He placed his left hand on my right, which was on my lap. "Look, Ba—, Mitchell. I...I know you've had a lot...on your mind, inside, over the years. Now, you can curse me out all you want to. But I didn't want to come out here to argue or fight. I brought you here because it is great seeing you. I missed you, and I wanted to have a good time."

"Uh-huh. You *brought* me out here to have one more for the road."

"Say what?"

"You heard. 'Oh, well, he's gonna be angry at me because of the way I treated him, no question. But, hey, I'm still irresistible, and I was his first love, so he still must feel something for me. So all I'll have to do is remind him of those good times, how good *we* were together, even play 'For the Good Times' on my car stereo, let Al Green set the mood, and by the time he's had a few drinks, he'll do whatever I want him to — *again.*' "

"So…do you still feel something?"

I smiled. "No."

He laughed. "Why don't *I* believe that…?" He signaled for the bartender.

"Because you don't want to."

He lifted his empty glass. He was drinking red wine. "I'll have another, and—" he turned to me "—would you like another refreshment?"

I pushed my empty glass forward; I had cranberry juice. "No. I've had enough, thank you."

"Uh, sure you wouldn't like to get *over-refreshed?*"

I got the joke. I grinned. "Yes. Yes, I'm sure."

We were silent as the bartender got his drink. After she left our end of the bar, he took my right hand.

"Mitchell...I know you don't believe me, I know you won't believe a word I say, but I'm going to say what I have to anyway."

I shrugged. "Okay. I'm listening."

He pondered his statement. He knew it had to be a good one. "You know that song by Sting, 'If You Love Somebody (Set Them Free)' "?

"Yeah."

"That's...that's how it was between us. I knew that...I knew that continuing what we had...you would need more than I could give. I could only be in your life for a short time. It was just for that time and place. It...it couldn't be more than that."

I didn't say a word. I went into the pocket of my spring jacket. I pulled out the card and handed it to him. He looked at it. He looked at me.

"You kept this all these years?" he asked.

"Yes."

"I thought you said you didn't feel anything for me...?"

"I don't."

"Well, why do you still have this?"

I took it from him. "To remind me."

"To remind you...of me?"

"No. To remind myself that...that my heart will be broken because sometimes promises won't be kept. In real life people say one thing, and then they do another."

"Hmm...sounds like a song." It is: another Randy Crawford standard.

"But even though that can happen, that doesn't mean you become so cynical, so skeptical, so jaded that you never allow yourself to love again."

"So what are you saying: that that is what I did to you?"

"Well, no. But that could very well have been me if I wasn't as strong as I was. And *that* you were responsible for."

"I was?"

"Yes. What, you didn't think my mental faculties were enhanced by all that body shaping you were doing with and to me?"

He looked at me. He shook his head. He sipped his wine.

"Not only did my body become stronger, but my mind did too. And not only did I begin to learn how to love another man, I learned how to love *me*. If I hadn't been somewhat sure of who I was and what I was — and who and what I wanted to become — I would've been destroyed by your shutting me out of your life. But I was able to survive it.

"So I guess, in a way, you're right: You were in my life, you could only be *in* my life for a certain amount of time. The journey I've taken since then, discovering and defining who I am as a same-gender–loving man, couldn't have happened with you — especially since you weren't taking that trip."

He placed his drink on the bar. "Say what?"

"Not once during the two years we were involved did I ever hear you say the words 'gay' or 'homosexual.' "

"That's because whatever I may be is none of your damn business."

"Well, it *is* my business — I should have made it my business. I had a lot of questions about myself, about you, about us, about life — about *the* life. But would you have answered them? I don't think so. Ha, your reaction to my query tells me that you wouldn't have been *able* to answer them. And because you knew we were getting to that point…what we had had to end."

I was obviously speaking the truth — he didn't have anything to say. He signaled for another drink. He placed his elbows on the bar.

I leaned forward. "You see…I'm involved with someone right now who is where I was ten years ago. But I'm not going to build him up to let him down. I'm not going to use his being naive, his being vulnerable, his being anxious, curious…against him. I'm not going to tell him that I love him because that's what he wants to hear or it's a convenient thing to say. And I'm not going to love him and leave him — especially when he needs me the most."

He sighed. He picked up his fourth drink, guzzled half of it, and turned to me. "So…who *is* this lucky person?" he groaned.

I went into my pants pocket and pulled out my wallet. I placed the photo of Pooquie and Junior on the bar. He picked it up. He studied them and studied me.

"Hmm…you all make one cute family." He handed the photo back to me. He took another big gulp. "He…he is lucky to have you."

"*I* am lucky to have *him*. To have *them*." I smiled at the photo. I placed it back in my wallet and returned the wallet to my pocket. "So you robbed me of some things. But not my capacity to love."

"I *robbed* you?"

"Yes, robbed."

He laughed very loudly. It was his Vincent Price sneer. "And just what did I rob you of?"

"Well, my virginity, for one."

"One cannot rape the willing. I didn't force you to do anything you didn't want to."

"No, you didn't rape me — even though the law would've seen it differently — but you did take my love, knowing that what I gave you you wouldn't give back."

"Uh-huh. And what else did I rob you of?" he smirked.

I sighed. "A dream."

He sucked his teeth. "A dream? What dream?"

"You don't even remember, do you?"

He shrugged, unconcerned. "If I did, I wouldn't be asking."

"I wanted to become a teacher."

He froze; he was about to chug down the last of his wine. He turned to face me. "A teacher?"

"Yes. A teacher."

He grinned. "Well, you certainly had one hell of an example in me."

"You think so, hunh?"

"Ha, I don't think so, I *know* so. You said so yourself. What was it? Oh, I helped you to get in touch with yourself, to appreciate yourself, to *love* yourself."

"Uh-huh. But look at the price I paid for it. I wanted to be a teacher since I was in the second grade. But when you cast me out of your life…I don't know. I guess subconsciously I saw that as a sign that this was a profession that I couldn't go into. After all the years of trusting, even caring for my teachers, you ruined that. And so I stayed away from it. I didn't realize it then, but I do now."

He slumped back in his stool. "Hmm…I am just responsible for everything that went wrong in your life, hunh?"

"No, not everything. Just a couple of things."

"So, what, am I supposed to apologize for that too?"

"No. I have to apologize to myself. I shouldn't have allowed what went down to prevent me from pursuing my lifelong goal. And I don't intend to anymore."

"Meaning?"

"Meaning, it's about time I reclaim that dream. Bring some integrity back to the profession."

He cut his eyes at me. "Ha, ha, ha. Very funny."

"Who knows…maybe I'll come back to Murrow."

"Oh, really? Hmm…I would love that."

"I'm sure you would. But I wouldn't be there for your enjoyment. I'd be there to keep my eye on you."

"And why would you need to do that?"

"After what I've been through with you and

what I saw tonight? You better hope somebody else doesn't have you under surveillance."

"You are just so preoccupied with Pierce, aren't you?"

"Well, I'm glad one of us is. You *should* be thinking about him right about now anyway. Did I not hear you tell him that you would be back?"

"So what, I don't come back. He is a big boy. He knows how to find his way home."

"That's not the point, and you know it."

"Look, I don't want to end this night on a sour note. Let's talk about us."

"Us?"

"Yes. Us. That is, so long as you've gotten everything out you needed to."

"Okay. And if I have...?"

He got close again. "The night is still very young."

This one I couldn't resist. "Warren, the *night* may be young...but *you* aren't." I eased up off the stool and out of his grasp. "I really have to be going."

He got up, struggling to get some money out of his pockets. "Wait, just wait, all right?" He threw three tens on the bar. He walked over to me and grabbed both my hands. "*He* will have you tomorrow and every day thereafter. We've only got tonight. *One* night. Is that a lot to ask? Look, we don't have to go to my place, we don't have to go *any*place. We can just walk around or just sit in my car and watch the sun come up. Please, Mitchell. Whatever you want to do, whatever you want me to do. I'm just trying to make it up to you. Please."

This was the moment I had been waiting for for ten years. He was actually begging to spend a few more moments with me. I could almost hear the desperation in his voice, the fear of rejection. The shoe was on the other foot. What a pity. How pathetic.

"Yes, there is something you can do for me," I answered after a rather long pause.

He became excited. He smiled. "Whatever it is, you got it."

I smiled. "You can hail me a taxi."

His face dropped. "What?"

"You can hail me a taxi. It's going on 1:30, and I have a very early and busy day coming up."

He knew he had been defeated, struck down in the final round. He knew it would be futile to fight anymore. He sighed. He squeezed my hands. "All right. Let's go." We nodded. I grabbed my jacket; he grabbed his blazer.

He immediately hailed a cab as soon as he stepped out into the street. He opened the door, leaning on it. I stepped around him to enter it.

He bent down inside the taxi. "Is this good-bye?" he asked.

I sat up; our lips were a few inches apart. "What do you think?"

"It...it doesn't have to be."

"I think you know it does." I kissed him on the cheek. "Thanks for the drink. Thanks for this chance. And thank you for the chance."

"I'll...miss you...again."

"Don't worry. There'll be a reunion in another ten years."

He frowned. He stood up. He closed the door. I told the driver where to go. We sped off. I didn't look back.

When I got home I went straight into the kitchen, where it was waiting for me. I took the card out of my jacket pocket and placed it in the dish. I picked up the matchbook on the counter. I lit a match and placed it in the center of the card. I went into the refrigerator and took out the glass of chardonnay. I lifted it up over the smoke and brooding fire.

"Here's to what once was...and what will be."

I sipped. I turned off the kitchen light, sat on the step stool, and watched it burn.

By the time I took my last sip, there was nothing but ashes left.

What Goes Around…

Four months later…

Pooquie and I were sitting up in bed, me
between his legs. We had finished watching
New York Undercover. He doesn't like watching
the show because he knows *I* love watching
Malik Yoba strut his sexy stuff each week (you
know I absolutely *gasped* when I interviewed
him for *New York Newsday*; he's even more
p-h-y-n-e in person). I usually tape it and view
it when Pooquie's not in. But he made an exception this time — and for a very jood reason: He
was on it.

He got the role thanks to the work of Troy
Fauntleroy, who turned out to be a miracle

worker for Pooquie. Because the few Black agents handling models didn't seem to be interested in him, Pooquie decided to give Troy a chance. Troy's game plan was simple: "You're big, you're bald, and you're Black. You're in vogue, so let's exploit it before you are *en vague*." He had never worked with a model, but his offer was hard to pass up: 10 percent instead of the standard 15 and no fee until he secured a job (he was so sure of himself that he shelled out the money to have pictures of Pooquie taken).

We weren't expecting to hear from him for some time, but two days after those photos came back, he sent Pooquie contracts for Macy's and Modell's. He's become a regular face in their weekly circulars as well as their commercials. And now he's blowin' up all over the place. In August he was tasting that long-lasting freshness of Big Red and shaving the few hairs on his chin with a Norelco blade. Last month he was scrubbing that beautiful body from head to toe with Zest and pumping iron on a Soloflex. He recently did his first *EM* shoot and got the chance to walk the runway in a Karl Kani show (not surprisingly, B.D. and I enjoyed this more than he did). He has an audition to occasionally appear as an "extra" (i.e., blackground) on *All My Children* tomorrow afternoon and just got word he'll soon be chomping on Pringles and chowing down on Big Macs. And because of all this exposure, Troy has put All-American jeans on notice: If they expect to hold on to Pooquie when his contract is up in a year, they better come high or stay home (they've gotten the message: Pooquie just received a nice cash bonus and will do his first All-American commercial in a few weeks).

Yeah, Troy has been earnin' his keep.

Pooquie's acting debut was a bit part as a college student (which, as I reminded him *again*, was yet another omen). He only had eight lines, and his screen time was no longer than three minutes, but what he had to say was important to the case detectives Williams and Torres had to solve. Yeah, he was great — and I showed him how much I loved his performance by doing a little performing of my own.

After I roxed his box, I went over the last few essays from my sixth-grade writing class at Knowledge Hall, an Africentric school a few blocks from our house. As I read and wrote, he watched me and watched the TV — even though the sound was down so it wouldn't disturb me.

I laughed. "This child is just too much."

"Who?" he asked, holding me tighter.

"Who else?"

"Willoughby?"

"Yes, Willoughby." I lifted the paper up so he could see it. " 'I know this essay is supposed to be about my goals for the future. But if I had my way, I would want to go back to the past. See, there's a lot of things I would want to do so that life could be better for the peoples today. You know, like tipping off the cops about James Earl Ray being on that rooftop. Or helping Harriet Tubman build some *real* tracks so that more of us could escape to the North and Canada. Yo, if they had the L train back then, there would've been no *need* for a Civil War!' "

We laughed.

" 'But the one thing I would really want to do is turn back that clock so I could talk to my mother. She died when I was just one. I don't remember her, but I remember the way she felt and being held by her. And I remember the way she smelled. But I can't see her face. I want to be able to see her and hold her the way she held me when I was a baby. I would want to know everything about her from her. It's not the same, with everybody else telling you what she was like.' "

191

Pooquie grinned. "Yo, that brotha is *too* tuff. And *deep*."

"Yes, he is. But once again he didn't do the assignment."

"C'mon, Baby, he did what he felt."

"Pooquie, it's not about what he *feels* like doing, it's about what he is *required* to do. Sometimes — many times in this life — what he'll want to do and what he's asked to do will be two different things, and he's gotta understand that."

"So you gonna give him an F?"

"No." I put a red *C* on the top of the paper.

His face said it all — a C ain't jood enough — but he told me anyway. "Oh, come on, now, Baby! Don't give tha brotha no *C*."

"Pooquie, I'm being rather generous. I know it took a lot for him to write this, and I know what he wrote came straight from the heart. But this was not the assignment I gave, and it wouldn't be fair to the other students."

"*You* ain't bein' fair, Baby."

"I'm not?"

"Nah. Givin' him a C just be-cuz he ain't express himself tha way you wanted him ta ain't right."

"That's not what I'm doing."

"You is too, Baby. When you think about it, he really did do whatcha asked him ta."

"How you figure?"

"Look at it this way: Tha only way he can really have plans fuh tha future is if he deals wit' his past. So he was tryin' ta get there by dealin' wit' his feelings about his moms. You tha one who said he be actin' out ta get attention. That's all a part of that."

I smiled. "Mmm. Ya know what?"

"What?"

"*You* are just *so* brilliant."

He grinned. "I know."

I kissed him. "Okay, okay. I'll compromise. I'll give him a B minus. How does that sound?"

He nodded. "Jood."

I made the change and added my comments. "But we're gonna have to have a discussion about his being more focused again. There can't be one set of rules for him and another for everyone else. But his talent *does* speak for itself."

"It sho' do. That rap he wrote was off tha hook."

"Yeah, it was. And speaking of dealing with things from the past: Did you call back Grampy Rivers?"

He sighed. "Yeah, I did."

"So… ?"

He stared at the TV. "We…gonna go out this weekend someplace."

"Does that *we* include Junior?"

"Nah."

"No?"

"No. But I'm gonna let him talk ta him."

"You are?"

"Yeah."

"Hmm, I bet Junior's excited. He's only talked to him once, and he didn't know it was him. Will this phone call take place on Saturday?"

"Yeah."

"Hmm, that's nice. I know Grampy had his heart set on meeting him and cooking dinner for the both of you. But I'm sure he's all right with this. Talking to his grandson on his birthday will still be a great present."

He looked down. I grasped and rubbed his chin.

"It's okay, Pooquie. It's gonna take time."

He looked up. He nodded. I kissed him on the cheek.

I then glanced at the television before turning my attention back to the essays, and I froze. My eyes bugged.

Is that… ?

"Pooquie, turn up the volume, quick!" I demanded, nudging him with my elbow.

"A'ight, Baby, a'ight." He grabbed the remote on the nightstand.

"…and here's Penny Crone, in Brooklyn, with this exclusive report. Penny?"

"Thanks, Rosanna, I'm standing in front of the seventy-first precinct in the Crown Heights section of Brooklyn, where a teacher is being held for allegedly committing one of the worst sins of an educator — sleeping with one of his students.

"Police say the man, Warren Adolphus Reid, a 44-year-old native of Kansas City, Missouri, will be arraigned tomorrow on a variety of charges, including first-degree sexual abuse, several counts of sexual battery, sodomy, rape, and endangering the welfare of a child. Authorities say that a recent graduate of Edward R. Murrow High School in Midwood alleges that Reid, the school's gymnastics coach, pressured him to have a sexual relationship. The young man says Reid convinced him he had the talent to be an Olympic gold gymnast but that Reid wanted to become more than his coach.

"Even though the young man is now eighteen, he spoke to *The 10 O'clock News* with his father present on the conditions that his face not be shown and his voice be disguised mechanically."

I didn't like to play sports a lot. My father always tried to get me to. But Mr. Reid, he changed all that. I really enjoyed being a gymnast...but one day he asked me to have sex with him. He said this was his payment for training me to be a champion.

"The young man went on to say that he reluctantly agreed to do it, thinking it would be that one time. But the demands for sex continued, with many of the encounters apparently happening at Reid's home, in Jamaica, Queens. The young man says the encounters didn't end until he graduated.

"Even though he says Reid threatened to harm both him and his family if he ever told anyone, the young man eventually confided in his father, who brought him to the seventy-first precinct this morning. The alleged victim claims Reid bragged that he could — and would — replace him with another male student."

I didn't want this to happen to anybody else. I didn't want anyone to go through what I

196

did. This...he shouldn't be able to get away with what he did. Nobody should be treated that way by a teacher."

"But Marvin Bloom, Reid's attorney, says that his client is not a rapist."

"I believe the evidence will show that my client did not rape this young man. In fact, there are letters, witnesses to incidents that took place outside my client's home, and notes made in the young man's own diary that we will subpoena, which will prove that he was in love with my client, was upset that my client isn't gay and didn't feel the same way, created an imaginary relationship in his mind that never took place, and made threats against my client's life."

"But the young man's father says that such charges are both insulting and impossible."

"If my son did such things, if he wrote such a thing, if he conducted himself in a manner that was un-Christian-like, he was most certainly confused and seduced into such sacrilege. I have raised a son with the highest regard and respect for his Creator, and the only way he could be led down such a road of destruction and abomination is if this... I couldn't even call this molester, this ungodly and unholy being a

man, because a real man would not covet a child in that way... The only way this could happen is if my son were forced to. I allowed my son to go on trips out of state, thinking he was being well-cared-for, and he is taken advantage of, violated, recruited by a homosexual. It makes one wonder what exactly the teachers in our schools are being paid to do."

"Well, the young man's father and the parents of all New York City public school students will get an answer to that and many other questions regarding this case when the state superintendent of schools, Jerry Norton, and the board of education's chief of student welfare and safety, Mercedes Rosado, hold a news conference tomorrow morning at 10 at board of education headquarters. Ms. Rosado told Fox-5 late this afternoon that she wishes to assure the public that they are on top of this situation and that all schoolchildren in the system are in good hands. We will be at that conference as well as the arraignment of Warren Reid and will keep you posted on any new developments. Live in Crown Heights, this is Penny Crone, with this exclusive *10 O'clock News* report. Now back to you, Rosanna."

"Thank you, Penny. And stay tuned to Fox-5 for any other news regarding this breaking—"

Pooquie hit the mute button. He giggled. "Uh-huh. I betcha that motha-fucka ain't gonna be pushin' up on nobody no mo'. Ha, *he* gonna hafta be worried about that now!"

I was in shock, staring at the screen, but was still able to say something. "I...I knew I had seen him before."

"Who?"

"Pierce."

"Pierce? Who he?"

"That...young man."

"You mean tha guy makin' them allegations?"

"Yeah."

"How you know who it is? They ain't show his face."

I leaned back against his chest. "Well, they practically told us everything about him except his name."

He squeezed me. "So you know him?"

"Uh, kinda. He goes to my church. Well, the church I *used* to go to. I hadn't seen him in years until that night at the reunion. He was there, working as a volunteer. And his father...I would recognize that self-righteous finger-pointing and self-hating propaganda anywhere."

"Wait, wait, hold up… You mean his pops is that preacher who was pushin' up on you years ago?"

"Yeah."

"And now he claimin' a coach done turned his son gay?"

"Yeah. Ain't that funny?"

"*Funny?* Yo, that shit is *wack*! But, hey, it's like they say: What goes around comes around. Fuh him *and* that fuckin' coach." He nudged me with his chin.

I sighed. "Yeah. I guess it does."